The Rope

C. T. Sahyer

Lloyd & Barb,
The best two friends a guy could ask for. Don't catch all the fish, leave some for me!

Clyde T. Sahyer
6-17-08

Eloquent Books
New York, New York

Copyright 2007
All rights reserved. C.T. Salyer

No part of this book may be reproduced or transmitted in any form or by any means, graphic, electronic, or mechanical, including photocopying, recording, taping, or by any information storage retrieval system, without the permission, in writing, from the publisher.

Eloquent Books
An imprint of Writers Literary & Publishing Services, Inc.
845 Third Avenue, 6th Floor – 6016
New York, NY 10022
www.eloquentbooks.com

ISBN: 978-1-934925-68-3 / ISBN/SKU: 1-934925-68-3

Printed in the United States of America

Cover Design: Mark Bredt
Cover photos: ©Ron Kacmarcik, ©Helder Almeida
www.DreamsTime.com

This book is dedicated to my loving mother and father, Clyde and Loretta. Without their support and encouragement this book would have never been written.

"Mom and Dad"
I love you both very much.

In Loving Memory -- John Oats
A treasured friend for over forty odd years

"John"
I miss you buddy.

Foreword

In the early sixty's in the suburbs of Orange County, Southern California, there lived a group of teenagers that the local cop affectionately called the Crew.

Being children of the cold war we always seemed to be searching for a little peace and tranquility. We'd gather on weekends, holidays or anytime we could get away from school (and our parents) to someplace quiet.

We could be roasting marshmallows around a campfire in the local mountains, burning hot dogs at the lake, waiting for the grunion to run, or watching the submarine races at the beach with our girl friends. One thing was assured, when the music was low and we ran out of things to talk about, Terry would start telling a story.

Now, forty years later the crew still gathers once a year for a reunion and Terry still keeps us entertained with his tales. You are invited to partake in a wonderful tradition

If you're close to the pool, the lake or the beach, open a cold one, put on some extra sun block, put your feet up and relax.

If it is cold, raining or snowing, put a log on the fire, pour yourself a glass of wine, curl up on the couch and get comfortable.

If you're on a plane, a bus or just passing time, you're in for a treat.

Picture yourself next to a campfire with some of your closest friends. The stars are out, its warm and everything is right with the world...

Now let go and let my brother Terry spin you a yarn.

Oh, by the way... Welcome to the Crew.

Rab

Chapter 1

It was still early morning when I reached the old wooden docks of the marina. The sun had not yet come up over the tree line across the river, but the light it was already giving off let me see that it was going to be a very special day. It was cool, but that added a pleasant reality to my excitement. I could feel the heaviness of the early morning air, as I walked down the long narrow wooden walkway. I could see her at the end of the dock. She was sitting there waiting patiently for my arrival and looked as pretty as the morning flowers that dotted the banks of the Mississippi river. In just a few short minutes she would be mine. She would be my very own houseboat and I would be her captain. Tom, the original owner of the houseboat, was already there. He would be giving me the keys to my dream and officially starting my retirement. I knew in my heart that this was going to be a wonderful day. This would literally be the first day of the rest of my life.

I had looked at many houseboats over the period of the last six months, keeping in mind that I would probably be spending the rest of my life aboard the one I chose. It had always been my dream to spend my golden years living on the water and traveling up and down the Mississippi river exploring all the wonders that it had to offer. Not only would I be able to travel to different places and experience different cultures, but I could also stop and fish, which was my real passion, any time the mood struck me. I would also be away from the stress and hassle of the city life that I had come to hate with a passion. But what really caught me by surprise was the cost of my dream. Financially, I was in pretty good shape. But the houseboats that made you feel like you were in a real home were way too far out of my price range. I had to settle for more like a nice trailer on pontoons than a floating house. Nevertheless, I was more than happy with my choice of the houseboat I bought. The boat I purchased from Tom was ten foot wide and forty-eight foot long. She had a full bedroom with a small bathroom and shower. There were also two queen size loft beds above a nice-size combined living and dining room with a full galley. There was a very nice uncovered rear deck, which had a green indoor-outdoor carpet covering it. It also had a large covered front deck with a veranda like patio and hard wood flooring. Both decks had iron railings with a hard wood varnished cap. Everything on board was electrical from the stove to the hot water heater. The electricity came from solar panels located on the roof above the loft beds. She was everything I needed and being a "Pirates of the Caribbean" movie fan and an adventurer/pirate in my own heart, I named her, "The Black Pearl."

Tom lived in Helena, Arkansas right on the west side of the Mississippi river. I had found the houseboat listed on the Internet back in December. Tom and I had talked many times over the phone and he had sent me many pictures of the boat, before I finally decided to buy it in late January. This was the first time I had met Tom in person and after thanking him again and taking possession of the Pearl, I turned the key, started the engine and pulled out onto the Mississippi river. I headed south down the river towards Greenville, Mississippi. I had taken a bus up the night before from there, where I had bought a small piece of property right on the river. It had a dock, garage, and storage shed to house my SUV and personal belongings. I would be using that as a homeport. As the Pearl and I cruised along with the

The Rope 3

current I slid a Charlie Pride CD into the CD player and helped him sing, "Roll on Mississippi" as we made our way towards Greenville. In my mind, life could not have been any more satisfying than it was at that moment.

It took a couple of days in Greenville, to get my personal belongings on board and set up banking and other accounts that I could access via the Internet from wherever I might wind up. I had a satellite system installed that would give me an Internet connection as well as television. I was proud of myself for finding a satellite dish that automatically tracked the satellite without my having to move the dish every time I stopped. It was expensive, but well worth it. When I thought the Pearl was completely set up, just the way I wanted it, and stocked with all the supplies and tackle she could hold, I started out on the adventure of my life.

My plan was simple. I would head south down the Mississippi like Huck Finn until I reached New Orleans. Stopping when I wanted to, and exploring all that the river had in store. If I hit a good fishing spot I might stay a day, or a week, depending on how I felt. I would be in no hurry. If I got bored I might stop and have dinner in one of the towns I passed along the way or maybe a drink or two at a local bar. After I was through with the Big Easy, I would head north again and go as far as the Mississippi would allow me to. I had no idea how long this journey would take but I had all the time in the world, so it didn't matter. My plan was working great. Over the next few weeks I caught a lot of fish, met a few nice people, and learned how to just plain relax.

One morning, as the Pearl lay anchored next to the bank, I was awakened by the sound of a barge hand singing out, "Quarter Less Thyree." I jumped out of bed, threw on my housecoat and ran out onto the front deck. There, across the river was a long string of barges being pushed up the river heading north. The barge hand was on the lead barge throwing a long line out ahead of him into the muddy water of the river. The line had different colored ribbons attached at certain intervals. As the line would come back to him, he would pull it tight and the ribbons would tell him the depth of the river at that spot. Then he would literally sing that information back to the boat pilot. As I remembered the stories that my father had told me, I knew exactly what information the barge hand was giving the boat pilot. Thyree was a very melodic expression of the number three. Quarter Less Thyree meant that the water there was three fathoms deep, less one quarter of a fathom. That meant the water was sixteen and a half feet deep.

The barge hand was just pulling the line tight once more as I heard him sing out, "Mark."

I waited in anticipation as he threw the line again. Then, after all of my fifty-seven years, I heard for myself one of the things that had captivated me by my father's stories about the river.

The barge hand sang out, "Mark, twain."

I started laughing aloud with excitement. If there had been any one else around they would have thought I had lost my mind. But I knew exactly what the barge hand had just relayed back to the riverboat pilot. The river was twelve feet deep at that spot. My father had told me how he used to throw that line as a young man when he was a barge hand and what the different depths were called. It was also the singing of that particular depth that the barge hand had just sang out, that made Samuel Clemens choose the pen name he took as a writer. I never did know if Samuel Clemens actually worked as a barge hand, as my father had, but I could not help but think of my dad just then and wished he was there with me at that moment. I would remember this morning for the rest of my life. It became one of many events that would validate my reasons for wanting to retire on the river. I walked back into the cabin, turned on the shower and began my day.

As my adventure continued down the Mississippi River, I thought to myself that the trip from Greenville to New Orleans would probably have only taken a couple of days, if I had been inclined to hurry. But I was not, and as it turned out it took me a little over two weeks to get there. I arrived in New Orleans just as the sun was going down. The lights of the city on both sides of the river lit up the sky so bright there was no need for lights on the Pearl for me to see my way. I could hear the sounds of music and partying coming from everywhere. The loud sounds of celebration made me feel as if I were coming into a giant festival of some sort, rather than a city. Mardi gras should have ended a couple of days ago but, I thought to myself, *maybe the partying is still going on*. It didn't matter to me either way. I knew I was going to enjoy myself while I was there.

I had no trouble finding a marina to moor The Black Pearl. It was still quite early and after paying the mooring charges, I headed into town on foot. I was a little concerned about being alone and walking the streets of New Orleans because of stories I had heard about the dangers there, on the news and in books I had read. I was very pleasantly surprised however, at how friendly the people were and how comfortable they made me feel.

I spent the next three days eating, drinking, and soaking up the *Big Easy*. It was great. The days flew by, and it was on the third night that I met Frank and Charlie at a popular little bar called *Pauline's Cajun Pub and Grub*. They were a couple of regular guys that were as in to fishing as I was. They told me about Lake Borgne, just east of New Orleans that had the biggest Redfish and Speckled Trout I could ever hope to catch. The lake was a large saltwater lake that opened up into the Gulf of Mexico. They told me that if I got lucky I might even catch a large Flounder or Halibut. I was definitely intrigued. Fishing was what my retirement was all about.

Frank went to his car and brought back an old dirty map that showed a canal that intersected with the Mississippi River just south of where we were. The canal headed north, and then turned east taking it up over the top of the lake. There was a channel that came off of the canal that headed south and dropped into Lake Borgne. I decided immediately that I had to fish that lake.

Later, I wished I had studied the map a little longer, or maybe not have had that last margarita. But, that was my plan, and I was sticking to it.

Chapter 2

The next morning I woke up with the worst hangover I've ever had. The fun I had last night didn't seem to be as enjoyable this morning. I didn't drink that much as a rule, but the margaritas had been very sweet and had gone down way too easy. I had enjoyed the evening laughing with Frank and Charlie and talking about fishing. However, it was obvious to me this morning that it had gotten a little out of hand. The sun was well above the point I had thought it would be upon my departure. I squinted at the clock through bloodshot eyes and realized it was almost noon.

If the mooring charges had been a little less, I might have stayed another day just to recover from last night's party. Funds were getting low and I decided that to stay would just be throwing money away. I stumbled into the shower and let the warm soothing water flow over my body for the next ten minutes. As I dried, then dressed, I was almost feeling human again. I lit a cigarette and walked out onto the front deck. I asked the attendant to fill both fifty-gallon fuel tanks as I stepped onto the dock and walked up to the store to stock up on some needed extra supplies. Three cases of beer, a fifth of rum, and a large bottle of aspirin were extremely high upon the list of items I knew I would need.

As I pulled away from the dock and headed the Pearl south, I opened a can of beer to begin my recuperation. I didn't normally drink during the day, but I had always heard that the best way to get over a hangover is to have a little hair of the dog that bit you. This would require a very large dog.

I traveled south constantly looking for the canal that would take me to the lake. As I traveled down the river, I suddenly remembered that I had a cousin that lived in New Orleans. I hadn't seen Mike in many years and thought to myself that I should have made an effort to look him up sometime in the last three days. I was sure I could have found him in the phonebook. I made a mental note to do that on the way back.

I saw the canal well before I got to it. I was relieved, I had ample time to traverse the traffic on the river and make my turn north. As soon as I had entered the canal I became aware of the fact that I was now going against the current and my speed was much slower. Even though I had no set time to get to the lake, I knew now that it would be dark long before I got there. I had never tried to travel at night. I had always anchored well before sunset. However, there were concrete levies on both sides of the canal, and no trees or debris to run into, so I didn't think it would be a problem if I had to travel a little bit after nightfall. I popped the top of my second can of beer and turned on the CD player as I continued up the canal.

I knew that I really shouldn't be drinking beer while piloting a boat, but the golden elixir was most definitely helping the hangover. As Waylon sang about honky-tonk women I started feeling a little better and hummed along. Within a few more songs and a couple more beers I had all eight speakers on the boat rocking to the music and was singing along in perfect harmony. I was feeling much, much better now and the beers were going down much, much faster. As the sun started to set I flipped on the front lights, illuminating the empty canal in front of me. The lights of the Pearl lit the way through the darkness better than I had ever hoped they would. I was feeling great and knew I could drive all night if need be. The only sound for miles around was the hum of the engine and Waylon and me singing, "Our heroes have always been Cowboys."

I was really enjoying myself now. Time flew by very quickly and it was about nine o'clock. The sun had been down for hours when I realized that the concrete levy on the right side of the boat had disappeared. It had changed into a dirt bank with trees and shrubs. As I pressed forward, every now and then I could see a pair of eyes staring out of the bushes and trees towards the boat. I laughed to myself and said out loud, "They're probably only something that wants to have me over for dinner."

As Waylon and I sang, and the solitary party continued, I suddenly saw it off to my right side. I was almost past the channel leading off to the south that leads to the lake. I spun the wheel hard right as fast as I could. The limbs of a tree that hung over the water on the left side of the channel scraped up against the Pearl as I barely made the turn in time. I steered the Pearl to the center of the thirty-foot wide stretch of water and started on another can of beer as my good friend Waylon and I sang about Luckenbach, Texas.

After traveling down the channel for about half an hour, and starting to see everything in duplicate, I thought to myself that it would probably be a good idea to bring the Pearl to a stop for the night and enter the lake in the morning. I steered my lady as close to the right side of the channel as I could, killed the engine, and dropped the anchors. After a couple more beers and a few more songs, I said goodnight to Waylon, turned off the CD player, and stumbled into bed.

The next morning I woke up realizing that I was still in the same clothes from last night. At least I had pulled off my shoes before I fell into bed. There had been no hard liquor like there had been at Pauline's, so I didn't feel as bad as I probably should have. But it was still apparent to me that I had partied a little more than I had meant to, just to clear the hangover from the night before last. Now, I enjoy beer as much as the next guy. Still, it was unlike me to have gotten plastered two nights in a row. A nice hot shower was definitely what the doctor would be ordering this morning. I grabbed a cola from the refrigerator and started peeling my clothes off. The soda was gone before the water even got hot. I jumped into the warm soothing water of the shower and thought to myself, "Man, does this feel good!" I could feel life pouring back into my body as the warm, clear liquid cascaded down over me. After the shower and clean clothes, I felt like a new man, ready to take on the world.

As I walked into the kitchen to grab another soda, I saw it out of the corner of my eye. My heart jumped up into my throat as I leaped backwards, dropping the can to the floor. Through the sliding glass doors, I could see it slithering across the front deck. It was a snake... it was a big snake... it was a very big snake. I hate snakes. They scare the hell out of me. I ran to the sliding glass doors and made sure they were locked. As I backed away from the doors I thought to myself how dumb it was to think the snake could actually open the door. Nevertheless, I ran throughout the boat and checked all the windows and the back door just to make sure they were all closed and locked. As I returned to the living room I just stood there and watched the snake slide slowly across the deck. It's tongue flickering out, tasting the air. I could feel my legs shake and my heart was beating twice as fast as it should. For a moment I thought I was going to be ill. I lit a cigarette and sat down at the kitchen table never taking my eyes off the giant scaly serpent.

I had no idea what kind of snake it was. It was just long and black. I didn't know if it was poisonous or not. I didn't really care. I just knew that, hopefully, I wasn't going to find out. I sat there for a long time smoking one cigarette after another wondering what to do. Finally I decided that if I didn't bother the snake maybe it wouldn't bother me. I stood up and walked towards the helm and started the engine. The snake obviously didn't like the sudden vibration of the engine and quickly slithered over the

The Rope

edge of the deck back into the muddy water of the channel. I never sighed a more satisfying breath in my life as I did just then.

My knees were still shaking as I flipped the switch and raised the anchors. I couldn't wait to get out of there. I steered for the center of the channel and pushed the throttle to three quarters ahead. My heart was still racing a few minutes later, as I throttled back and came to a more comfortable cruising speed. I don't know why snakes affect me in that way, but I prayed I wouldn't run into any more.

As I cruised along I noticed that the channel had slowly turned from a southerly direction to a more west-by-southwest direction. That didn't make any sense to me. The map I had looked at back at Pauline's indicated that the channel went straight south for a very short distance and dumped immediately into the lake. I calculated that, with the distance I had traveled down the channel last night and now this morning, I had gone about six or seven miles. Something was wrong. I brought the Pearl to a stop and turned on the computer. I was going to look up a map of the lake on Google, but the computer said it had no Internet connection. I got up and looked out the window. The trees on the south side of the channel were blocking the satellite dish from getting a signal.

I opened another soda as I pondered my situation. In my drunken stupor last night I had obviously turned onto the wrong channel. I made another mental note. No more drinking and driving. The channel I was on was only thirty to thirty-five feet wide with a thick forest of trees on both sides reaching up at least thirty feet high. The tops of the trees hung out over the channel almost touching each other in places creating a dark and somewhat spooky tunnel. The screeching of birds and other wild life gave it the feel of a hot and humid jungle. It was obvious that I couldn't turn a forty-eight foot-long boat around in such a narrow channel and I surely couldn't back up a forty-eight foot-long boat for seven miles. I reached up and turned on the CB radio. I flipped the dial around to all forty-two channels, but didn't hear any chatter on any of them. I spent the next thirty minutes yelling, "Breaker, breaker" on all the channels especially on channel nine the emergency channel, but with no response.

I walked over to the sink and picked up my cell phone from the countertop. It didn't come as any great shock to me that there was no signal. I walked over to the sliding glass doors looked out on the deck, checking for anything that might be slithering around. After I was pretty sure I was alone I unlocked the door and stepped out, my eyes scanning the deck and the canopy constantly for any movement. I walked all over the deck holding the phone up in the air waving it around like a fly swatter but still could not get a signal. Just then I heard a splash and turned to look down the channel just in time to see the tail of the first alligator, and then a second alligator, sliding off the bank into the channel. As serious as I have ever been in my life, I said out loud, "This is not good." Even though the sight of an alligator hadn't unnerved me the way the snake had, I knew I didn't care to be around either one. I walked back into the cabin, then closed, and locked, the sliding glass doors again.

When I first started this adventure the fact that I was doing this alone didn't seem to bother me too much. I had been alone for quite a few years now and was very comfortable with my own company. I always thought that if I did get lonely, I could always buy a dog. I wished the dog were here now. I opened the refrigerator and studied my options. Should I have a soda or a beer? I pondered the decision for what seemed to be a long time. Even though the other was more tempting, I chose the soda. I needed to keep a clear head until I decided what to do; besides, it was the beer last night that put me in this position to begin with.

I opened the can, lit a cigarette, and sat down at the table. I knew I needed to think this out rationally. There were enough supplies on the boat to last me quite awhile, three or four weeks at least, so that was not a pressing concern. I could just sit here and hope that someone came by and tell me where to go so I could turn the Pearl around. In my gut I knew that was unlikely. I had enough fuel onboard to go another two hundred fifty, maybe three hundred, miles. Surely, if I continued on, I would either find the lake or at least a large enough body of water to turn around in. If the channel turned back towards the south, or even the north, there might be a clear enough path through the trees for the satellite dish to get a signal and I could get a map, and maybe find a way out. I decided to keep going ahead and hope for the best. I stood up, walked over to the helm, and started the engine once more. As I throttled the Pearl foreword I promised myself that when I got out of here, I would buy a dog.

I traveled up the channel for about another two miles and noticed that it was still turning more towards the west. Up ahead, I could see that the channel forked off into two directions. Both channels appeared to be about the same width as the one I was on. I slowed down to a crawl to give myself a few more seconds to decide which one to take. The decision didn't come quickly. If I took the one to the left I would be getting farther away from where I had come in. Then again it might turn to the south enough for the satellite to get a signal and I could download a map. Whereas the channel to the right, might turn back to the north and take me back to the main canal. If it turned enough to the north I could get a map that way, also. I made my decision and throttled the Pearl forward heading towards the channel on the right.

I hadn't gone far when the channel took a sharp left then a sharp right turn. I came to another fork, except this time; there were three to choose from. Right, left, or straight ahead. Again, I chose the one on the right using the same theory as before. The channels were really starting to curve back and forth a lot now. I passed a couple channels that came off ninety degrees to the left and a few that came off ninety degrees to the right, but there was no chance of turning the Pearl that sharp into such a small channel. Each time I came to a fork, I took the channel to the right hoping that if I did find a place to turn around I would simply follow the channel back, taking the one to the left on my return.

The hours passed by very slowly as I tried to figure out all the possibilities of how to find my way back. Then it happened. I could see it up ahead. The channel was about to empty into a larger body of water. As I got closer I could see it was a lake. Not as large as the one I was looking for, but more than big enough to turn the Pearl around. Elation swept over me. I throttled up to full and charged the lake like a madman. As I drove out of the channel onto the lake I decided it would probably be a good idea to get far enough out so I could get a satellite signal and print out a map. The lake looked to be about a mile across so I headed for the northernmost shore. As I got there I decided that this would be a good place to stop for a while. I could get the map and something to eat. It had been a very long day and I needed to put something in my stomach.

As the Pearl came to a stop, I killed the engine and flipped the switch to drop the anchors. I walked over and pushed the button on the computer. My heart sang as I read "Connecting to the satellite." I knew it would take a few minutes so I opened the fridge and got out some ham to make a sandwich. I looked at my watch and saw that it was three thirty-five. It was still mid-February so I knew the sun would be going down between five-thirty and six. I wouldn't have enough time to make it back to the canal before dark. But I was on a lake and there were probably fish here. So I decided that after I got the map, I would anchor closer to the center of the lake and wait for morning to head back.

The satellite connection was complete. I laid the half eaten sandwich down and pulled up Google maps. As I zeroed in on the New Orleans-Lake Borgne area I could see where I had made my mistake. I had turned too soon. The channel that leads to

Lake Borgne was another twenty miles east of where I had turned. The channel I had taken put me smack dab in the middle of the Bayous and the swamps. I enlarged the map area of the Bayous and printed out a copy. I finished the sandwich as the printer clicked away. As I waited for the printer to finish I heard a splash off to the north side of the boat. I looked out the window and saw three alligators sunning themselves on the shoreline. I thought to myself that this would be a great time to move the Pearl out towards the center of the lake. I turned the key and started the engine.

I anchored the Pearl as close to the center of the lake as I could. Pointing it in the direction of the channel I would be taking in the morning. I made another sandwich, took the map and headed out onto the front deck scanning everywhere for anything that moved as I walked. Feeling that I was the only living creature on the boat, I sat down at the table to finish my lunch and study the map. As I looked at the printout I could see where I had left the canal and entered the channel. I could even see how it slowly turned towards the west and the first fork I had taken. But after that first fork it became confusing. Nothing looked like what I remembered as I had driven along. The channels on the map went everywhere. They were crisscrossing each other and winding every which way. I couldn't even tell which lake I was on. There were dozens of lakes that looked like this one all over the map.

I knew storms and, even more so, Hurricane Katrina could change the landscape easily, especially here in the Bayous. Who knew how old this map was? I remembered looking up my parent's house on a Goggle satellite map just a couple of months ago and seeing the motor home my parents had sold three years earlier sitting in the driveway. Even my GPS didn't help because there were no GPS indicators on the map. I made myself another promise. When I got out of here I would buy myself a dog and a current atlas of the United States that had GPS indicators on it.

I was taking the last bite of my lunch, still studying the map, when the movement in the water caught my eye. It was another snake. My throat almost closed and I almost choked on the sandwich. Thank God it was swimming away from the boat. I made myself another promise. When I got out of here, I would buy myself a dog, a current atlas of the United States that had GPS indicators on it and a shotgun. A very large-gauged shotgun. I wondered if it would be legal to mount a fifty-caliber machine gun on the front deck.

As the snake disappeared into the glimmer of the sun reflecting off the water, I decided that maybe a little fishing would help take my mind off things. I walked back into the kitchen, opened the refrigerator, and took some frozen shrimp from the freezer. I ran the frozen shrimp under the faucet as I popped the top on another can of cola. When the shrimp were thawed enough to put a hook through them, I carried the bait and the soda back out to the picnic table on the front deck. I took a fishing pole off the rack that was up against the cabin wall. It was a deep-sea fishing rod that my father had given me. I thought it would be perfect for catfish. I rigged the pole with three hooks and a fairly large weight. I baited the three hooks with the shrimp and cast it out into the lake. When it finally hit bottom, I reeled the line in until it was tight. I placed the pole in the holder that was on the railing, sat down at the table, and took a sip of my soda.

As I sat there I thought about putting some music on the CD player and maybe grabbing another cigarette. As I stood up to walk back into the cabin the pole bent over like a whip. I grabbed it out of the holder and jerked it upwards to set the hooks. It became clear, very quickly, that I had a very nice size fish on the line. It fought gallantly as I slowly raised the tip of the pole, then reeled as I lowered the tip back down. What ever it was, there was a lot of fight in him. It ran line out on me three times. As the fight continued I slowly adjusted the drag, giving

The Rope

the fish less chance to pull more line. Finally, after a good ten or fifteen minutes, it broke the surface. It was the largest blue channel cat that I had ever seen. Just guessing, I figured it weighed somewhere between twenty and twenty-five pounds. It had wrapped himself around the line and had all three hooks embedded in him. It wasn't about to get away with the eighty-pound test line I was using.

As I got the fish close to the boat I slowly backed up to the cabin wall. I put the handle of the pole between my legs and, holding on to it with one hand, grabbed the net off the cabin wall with the other. As I held the tip of the pole up with my left hand, I scooped the net under the fish with my other. I had it. I laid the pole down on the deck and with both hands on the net lifted the heavy catfish onto the boat. I was ecstatic. This was what it was all about.

I dragged the net with the catfish over to the center of the deck. The big cat was courageously flipping and turning trying to escape. I put my right knee on the fish's back to keep him still long enough to remove the hook in his mouth and the two he had rolled himself up in. When all the hooks were out, I shoved my right arm into the fish's mouth and grabbed him by the gills. I slowly untangled the fish from the net and carried the monster over to the cutting board on the cleaning table. I was sure, now, that the giant fish weighed all of twenty-five pounds.

As I lifted the large catfish onto the cutting board, the fish made one final attempt to get away. It flipped over on its back nearly breaking my right arm. It took all I had to flex my body up and over the table to keep the fish from snapping my arm in two. I had to use all my strength to flip the big cat back over on its stomach and pull my throbbing arm out of its mouth. My right arm was killing me as I held the back of the mighty fish with my left hand. Holding it down as hard as I could. I grabbed a large meat cleaver hanging on the hook below the cutting board and with one mighty blow to the back of the fish's head the fight was over. I left the cleaver buried halfway into the fish's neck and walked back over and sat down at the table. I was exhausted.

My right arm hurt severely. I cradled it gently on my lap and was rubbing it trying to ease the pain. I had caught catfish before, but never this large. It was common practice for me to handle that type of fish by grabbing its gills from inside its mouth. It's a good way to carry a cat, but next time I will make sure it's dead before I do, especially for a large fish like that. It took over an hour for my arm to quit hurting enough for me to get up and move around. It had been a gallant fight, and for the first time in my life, the fish had almost won the battle.

I finally stood up from the table. Still babying my arm. I went to the fridge and opened another soda. As I walked back out to clean the fish, I turned the CD player on and took a sip of the soda. It took me almost an hour to gut and fillet the large catfish. When I was finally finished, I carried the fillets into the kitchen and, after hunting for the zip lock bags, I bagged and placed them in the freezer. After straightening up the cleaning table and putting away my pole the sun slowly disappeared below the tree line on the west side of the lake. I spent the rest of the evening watching television and nursing my arm. When I finally went to bed, I had to sleep on my left side with my right arm hanging lifelessly over the edge of the mattress.

When I woke up the next morning and looked at the clock, it was a few minutes after five. The sun would be up pretty soon. I got up, flexing my still sore right arm as I jumped into the shower. After I had dressed and combed my hair, I walked into the living room and stared out the sliding glass doors. No company. I was relieved. The sun was not up over the trees yet, but it was light enough to get started. I fired up the engine and flipped the anchor switch. I put on a Shania Twain CD and headed for the channel I had entered the lake on yesterday afternoon. With any luck I would be back in New Orleans by early this evening.

As I approached the small cove that I had entered the lake from my heart sank. I brought the Pearl to a halt. In my excitement of finding the lake yesterday I had rushed onto it without checking the surroundings. As I sat there looking out the window I realized that my attention for details needed a lot of work. This could be bad. This could be really bad. I cut the engine and dropped the anchors. As I sat there in my captain's chair staring out the window in disbelief, I wasn't looking at one channel; I was looking at three channels. I had no idea which one I had entered the lake from. "Houston, we have a problem."

I walked over to the table and picked up the map. I tried to find a lake that had three channels coming off of it on the southeast corner. There were none. I knew that if I chose the wrong channel I could be wandering around lost for days. This was already the third day. It would take another full day just to get out of the swamps. That is, if I chose the right channel. I tried the cell phone and the CB radio again with the same results as yesterday. No signal and no one on. I thought about going to the center of the lake and sending an e-mail to my son, but where would I tell him I was? My son lived in Texas and it would probably just upset him more than it would do me any good. So after weighing all the options I decided just to trust my instincts and pick a channel. I had said I would go back following the left channel, so that was the way I decided to go. I started the engine and raised the anchors. I headed down the channel on the left.

I followed the channel southeast. Each time I came to a fork I chose the left one. There were a lot of forks and the channels twisted and turned all over the place. I passed a clearing on my left that appeared to be an old Cajun graveyard that I knew I had not seen on my journey yesterday. The thick green ivy that covered the grave markers gave me the impression that no one had been here for quite a long time. It didn't take long to realize that I had taken the wrong channel again. This time I really felt lost and the eeriness of the graveyard sent shivers down my back.

I reached over and turned the CD player off. Shania was getting on my nerves.

I had been traveling for hours when I came out onto another lake. It was much smaller than the one I had spent last night on, but it felt good to have some room around the boat. I pulled out towards the center and stopped the engine. I took the map and stepped out onto the front deck. I realized that it would do no good to just turn around and go back the way I had come. I scanned the lake and tried to find something on the map that looked like it. There were three or four that looked similar. I was getting very depressed now and thought to myself that I could really be in trouble. I could actually be lost out here for a very long time.

Chapter 3

The sun was directly over the top of the Pearl as I slowly scanned the lake. It was getting warm and the mosquitoes were now out in force. As a bead of sweat formed on my forehead and I swatted at one of the bloodsuckers on my arm, I noticed something on the other side of the lake that didn't quite fit in with the rest of the landscape. I walked back into the cabin and got my binoculars. As I brought the glasses into focus, I could see that it was a short wooden dock with a small boat sticking out from the tree line on the far side of the lake. I got excited again. If someone were there, maybe they could tell me how to get out of here. I ran back to the helm and started the engine. As I got closer, I could see what looked like the roof of a small house through the trees. I slowed the Pearl to a crawl, and then shut off the engine. I ran to the front of the boat and waited as the Pearl slowly drifted towards the dock. I jumped onto the dock and pushed on the nose of the Pearl until she came to a complete stop. I tied her off and headed up towards the house.

As I approached what looked like a very old and run down one room shack, I could see a woman sitting on the steps of the porch. As I got closer, the woman looked up and saw me. She jumped up with a frightened look on her face and ran into the shack with what looked like a rope attached to her right ankle. As I stepped up onto the porch, I could see one end of the rope tied to the post that held up the roof of the porch. The rope stretched into the shack through the doorway. Just then the smell hit me. It was awful. I had never smelled anything like it in my life. It was coming from inside the shack. It was the kind of smell that took your breath away. I pulled a handkerchief out of my back pocket and covered my mouth and nose as I reached the open door. I knocked on the wooden frame as I stuck my head into the shack. The woman that had been sitting on the porch was standing in the back of the shack near a bed, staring at me and shaking like a trapped animal. A man was lying on the bed, next to her, his eyes and mouth hung open, staring at the ceiling. His skin was dark gray, almost black, and it was apparent that he had been dead for quite some time. I motioned for the woman to come outside as I stepped back out of the doorway and off the porch to catch my breath.

I stood outside the shack for well over ten minutes before the woman cautiously appeared in the doorway. She was obviously frightened and didn't know what to think of my being there.

I lowered the handkerchief from my mouth and asked, "Are you all right?"

She stood there for a long time staring at me and the Pearl tied to the dock. She then shook her head up and down, indicating that she was okay.

I asked, "How long has the man inside been dead?"

There was another long pause and then she finally held up her hand with all five fingers extended.

I asked, "Five days?"

She shook her head up and down again then meekly asked, "Water?"

The woman was very thin and she looked like she had never seen a bathtub in her life. Her hair was stringy and full of mats. The thin cotton dress she had on was filthy and torn in many places. She was also barefoot. She looked to be in her mid-forties. Then, on top of it all, there was that rope around her ankle.

My attention snapped back to her question. "Water?" I asked, "I have plenty of water on my boat. Are you thirsty?"

She just mumbled, "Drink?"

I answered, "Sure, are you hungry?"

She shook her head up and down again indicating that she was.

I said, "Come on down to the boat and I will give you something to eat and drink."

She stood there for a moment looking scared and finally said, "Can't."

She looked down at the rope on her leg. I walked over to where she was standing to look at the rope wrapped around her ankle. She started to back up as I got close to her and started to turn her head from side to side, looking for a place to run. I stopped my approach and tried to assure her that I would not harm her. She seemed to calm down a little so I continued up to the edge of the porch. The rope wasn't tied, but rather looped and pulled snug around her ankle.

I looked up at her and asked, "Can't you take the rope off?"

The woman looked down at me and answered very quickly, "Oh no, can't take rope off."

I asked, "Why not?"

The frightened woman turned her head and looked back into the shack. "He hurt me if rope off," She replied.

I knew right then and there that I couldn't leave the woman here alone. She was starving, and very afraid of whomever the dead man in the shack was. So afraid that she couldn't understand the fact that he was dead and couldn't possibly harm her any more. I knew I would have to take her back with me. Surely someone in New Orleans could help her. That is if I could ever find my way back there.

I looked up at the woman and said, "Ma'am, I promise you, he can't hurt you any more" and I reached over and loosened the loop and let the rope fall to the porch floor.

The woman became terrified. She started breathing very heavily and was snapping her head back and forth in all directions looking for someone or something that might attack her. She jumped off the porch and grabbed me, still looking for the axe to fall from somewhere.

I put my arms around her and told her that she would be all right, that I would not let anything happen to her. It was hard to hold the woman close because she smelled so bad. I literally tried to hold my breath as I slowly walked her down towards the Pearl. I struggled as I held her up and helped her walk; she was very weak and stumbled repeatedly as we headed down the dirt path towards the dock. She held on to me very tightly still fearing something bad was going to jump out from somewhere and get her.

As we entered the cabin of the Pearl, I sat her down at the kitchen table. I took a glass from the cupboard and filled it with water. As I reached over to give her the glass, she grabbed it and started gulping down the liquid as fast as she could. I cautioned her to slow down. The glass was emptied in a matter of seconds. I took the glass and refilled it. As I handed it back to her, I told her to take her time, that I had plenty of water and she could have all she wanted. As she started on the second glass of water, I took out some ham from the refrigerator to make her a sandwich. When I handed it to her, she tore into it like she had with the first glass of water. She obviously had not eaten or had anything to drink in quite a while. I made her a second sandwich and filled the glass again.

As she ate, I flipped on the GPS and jotted down the coordinates of the shack location. Then I walked out onto the front deck and untied the Pearl from the dock. I walked back into the cabin and started the engine. The woman didn't seem to notice or be frightened at the sound or movement of the boat. She just seemed to only care about the food and water. I backed away from the dock and headed out to the center of the lake. I was still lost and had to figure out what my next move was going to be.

I looked at my watch; it was just past noon so I figured I had plenty of time to keep trying to find a channel that would lead me back to the canal. I decided that our best chance would be to scout the east side of the lake and, hopefully, find a channel that headed off to the north, or even better the northeast. I turned the wheel of the Pearl and headed for the east side. The woman was still eating, but she seemed to have calmed down quite a bit. She was eating much slower now and taking smaller sips of water. As she ate, she stared at me and watched my every move.

I looked over at her and said, "By the way, my name is Terry, what's yours?"

She swallowed the bite of sandwich she was working on and, after a long pause, she softly said, "Yu."

I thought to myself, "Was she Asian?" I responded, "It's nice to know you, Yu."

As we approached the east side of the lake, I saw a channel that headed straight off to the east. It was wider than most of the channels I had been on and, even though I would have preferred it to be heading in a more northeasterly direction, I decided it was better than nothing. I pushed the throttle forward and headed towards the channel.

I had only gone about a mile up the channel when Yu finished her sandwich. I decided to bring the Pearl to a stop and get the woman cleaned up. She smelled awful and was fouling the air in the entire cabin. As the Pearl slowly came to a halt, I flipped the switch and dropped the anchors. I walked into the bedroom and opened up one of the chest of drawers and then another. I was looking for a pair of sweatpants and sweatshirt that I had. I knew the blue jeans I wore would be too big for her and the pull string band on the sweatpants would probably work better around her tiny waist.

After searching through a couple more drawers I found them and laid them out on the bed. I also laid out a pair of my briefs and a pair of socks. I stepped into the bathroom and turned on the shower so that the water would get warm. I walked back into the living room and asked Yu to come with me. She slowly followed me into the bedroom. I showed her the clothes I had laid out and told her to just pile her dirty clothes on the floor. I would take care of them later. I gave her a clean washcloth and a bar of soap. I explained how to use them and then showed her the shampoo and conditioner for her hair. I laid out a fresh towel and told her to use it to dry off with when she was finished. It all seemed new to her, but she listened like she understood everything I was telling her. I closed the bedroom door and walked back up to the sliding glass doors and opened them as wide as they would go, trying to air out the cabin. I walked back over to the helm and started the engine once more and flipped the switch to raise the anchors. I put a Jim Croce CD on the CD player, pushed the throttle forward and headed the Pearl up the channel.

It was about twenty minutes later when the bedroom door opened, and Yu stepped out. As I turned back and looked at her, I couldn't help but think, "Man, what a difference." She looked ten years younger. I noticed for the first time that she was actually cute. In fact, she was very cute. The sweatpants and sweatshirt were a little baggy, but looked fine. I took a good look at her as she stood in the doorway. She was about five foot, five inches tall. She was very thin, weighing about a hundred pounds. Her hair was blonde and set off the most beautiful green eyes I had ever seen. Her hair was still wet and hung straight down and I noticed that she wasn't wearing the socks that I had laid out for her.

I asked her to come over and sit down at the table. As she took her first step, she started to stumble. I quickly let go of the wheel and grabbed her before she fell. I held her up, and half carried her to the kitchen chair. It was clear that she was still very weak. As she sat up in the chair and became more comfortable, she started looking around the cabin as if for something in particular it seemed. I realized she was looking to see where the music was coming from. I smiled as I stepped back over to the helm and throttled the Pearl back down until she came to a complete stop. I dropped the anchors again.

I decided to take a few minutes and try to make Yu more comfortable. I walked into the bedroom, picked up the dress that lay on the floor, opened the back door, stepped out onto the rear deck, and threw it overboard. Returning to the bedroom, I took the socks that I had laid out on the bed, grabbed my pair of house slippers, and walked back into the living room. I unfolded the socks and kneeled down to put them on her feet. She started to pull her feet away as I touched them, but then relaxed and let me put the socks on her. I then slipped on the house shoes and stood up. She looked at her feet for quite awhile, flexing them up and down to get the feel of the slippers. She looked up at me and smiled. She had a lovely smile. I thought to myself, "She likes them." I walked back into the bathroom and got my hair dryer and comb. Yu looked puzzled as I brought them back to where she was sitting.

I explained, "This is a comb and something to dry your hair with."

I ran the comb through my own hair, then plugged the hair dryer in and turned it on. Yu jumped back a little at the sound of the hair dryer, but I took her hand and blew the warm air across her arm to show that it would not hurt her. I then turned her around and gently ran the comb through her hair. I slowly started to add the warm air of the hair dryer. As she sat there, she slowly closed her eyes and a faint smile came across her face. I thought to myself that she was actually enjoying this. It took about five minutes to comb her hair out and get it all dry. I turned the hair dryer off and sat it, and the comb, on the countertop. Yu reached up and felt her hair and smiled as she looked up at me again. I reached into the refrigerator and took out two colas. I popped the top on one and set it in front of her. I then sat down across the table from her and opened mine.

Yu looked at the can of soda, as if to say, "What's this?"

I said, "It's a soda. A drink" and I tipped the can up to my mouth and took a sip.

Yu picked up her can and slowly lifted it to her mouth. Her eyes got real big and she smiled. She started gulping it down very quickly.

"I wouldn't drink that so fast," I warned, "It's carbonated."

Yu was still smiling real big as she lowered the can and said, "Goo...." then she belched very loudly.

I started laughing hysterically. Yu covered her mouth with her hand and looked shocked. She acted like she didn't know what to do, as if she might be in trouble or something. As she watched me laughing, she must have realized everything was all right and she started to smile.

Then she said in a very low voice, still covering her mouth with her hand, "Good."

I was still laughing as I stood up, took my drink and walked back to the helm. We had been parked long enough and it was time to get back to trying to find a way out of here. I started the engine and raised the anchors.

I looked over at Yu and said, "There are plenty of sodas in the refrigerator. You can have all you want, just drink them a little slower." I laughed again as I pushed the throttle forward and continued down the channel.

Yu was smiling as she looked up at the ceiling again and said, "I like."

As I guided the Pearl down the channel I responded, "That's Jim Croce. He's one of my favorite singers."

Yu was smiling even bigger now as she said again, "I like."

As we cruised up the channel, we both sipped our drinks and I could see Yu's head swaying back and forth as she listened to the music. I thought this might be a good time to ask her about the shack and her life there. I could see that she was enjoying herself however, probably for the first time in a long time, so I let it go. I could also see that her eyes were trying to close and she looked exhausted. It had been a very trying day for her so I made sure the Pearl was headed straight down the center of the channel. I flipped the small metal ring on the dashboard over the steering wheel to hold it in place and then took her hand and led her into the bedroom.

I patted the top of the mattress and said, "Why don't you lay down and listen to the music and try to get a little rest."

Yu stood there for a moment, looking at me like she didn't know what I wanted her to do. Then she slowly crawled upon the bed and laid her head on the pillow. I took off the slippers and pulled the bedspread over her. I walked back to the helm to continue down the channel. Yu was asleep before I even got the ring back off of the steering wheel.

The channel had narrowed and widened a couple of times over the next hour and had slowly turned to the left and was now heading in a more northerly direction. I glanced at my watch and said out loud, "Four-thirty".

It would be getting dark again soon. I didn't relish the idea of spending another night in the swamps. Yu had been asleep now for about an hour and a half, but I could hear her moving around like she might be getting up. I looked back towards the bedroom and saw her standing in the doorway.

She looked at me and quietly said, "Have to pee."

I checked my heading as I flipped the ring over the steering wheel and walked back to the doorway. I directed her into the bathroom and showed her how to use the pump toilet. I closed the bedroom door and headed back to the helm. Yu reappeared a few minutes later, walked to the kitchen table, and sat down. She was walking better now and seemed to be getting some of her strength back. She looked up at me, smiled, and just nodded her head up and down. I nodded back and thought to myself that she might be getting hungry again. I looked down the channel to make sure we were going straight and flipped the ring back onto the steering wheel once more. I opened the refrigerator and popped the top of a soda then handed it to her. Yu smiled widely as she took the can from me. I pulled out a couple of chicken potpies from the freezer and placed them in the toaster oven. I set the temperature to four hundred and turned the timer to forty minutes. I walked back to the helm and took the ring off of the wheel.

It was a couple of minutes after five when I noticed the channel was about to enter another lake. As we came out onto the lake I could see that it was a very large one, I couldn't see the other side of it. Just then I noticed a small outboard motor boat with two men sitting in it fishing, just a short distance from us.

"People," I yelled out loud.

I slowed the Pearl down to a crawl and headed towards the boat. As I got closer, I shut off the engine and ran out onto the front deck. Yu walked out with me, still clutching her soda. When she saw the two men in the boat, she quickly stepped back into the doorway, hiding from their view.

As the Pearl drifted closer to the boat, I yelled, "Howdy. Can you tell me what lake this is?"

The man in the back of the small boat yelled back, "Lake Borgne."

I got excited because I knew I wasn't lost any more.

I yelled again, "Is there a ranger station or a fish and game office anywhere on the lake?"

The man in the boat yelled back, "I don't know. But there is a marina on the north side of the lake. I'm sure they would know."

I asked, "How far is that?"

The Rope

The man in the boat yelled, "About twenty miles straight north of here."

The two men will probably never know how happy they had just made me.

I asked one more question, "Have you had any luck today?"

The man in the front of the boat bent over and lifted up six of the nicest Speckled Trout I had ever laid my eyes on. Frank and Charlie had not lied.

I yelled back, "Very nice. And thank you very much."

I waved goodbye to them as Yu and I walked back into the cabin. As I started up the engine, I could see the two men pulling up their anchor and getting ready to call it a day. I knew there was no chance of going twenty miles before it got dark so I pulled the Pearl out a little farther onto the lake and shut off the engine. I flipped the switch and dropped the anchors. The pot pies were almost done so I decided that we would eat and spend the night here. We would get an early start tomorrow morning and head for the marina.

I didn't think Yu had any idea why I was so happy. I honestly thought she was smiling just because I was. Yu watched as I ran to the linen cabinet and pulled out a tablecloth. I dashed out onto the front deck and covered the picnic table with it. I ran back in and grabbed two plates from the upper cabinet and some silverware from the drawer. I shuffled back outside and set the table. I came back in and grabbed a soda and a beer from the fridge and took them out to the table. If I had a candle I would've placed one of them out there also. I was feeling good.

I checked the potpies and figured they had about another five minutes to go. I escorted Yu out to the table and pulled her chair out for her to sit down. I realized that I had forgotten my manners, so I ran back into the cabin and grabbed a glass from the cabinet. I hurried back outside, opened Yu's drink, and poured it into her glass. I walked over and picked up my beer, popped the top, and extended the can towards Yu. She sat there for a second with a puzzled look on her face and then reached up to take the can. I laughed as I pulled the can of beer back. I reached over, picked Yu's glass up, and handed it to her. I then extended her arm towards me and clicked my can of beer against her glass.

"It's called a toast," I told Yu.

Then I took a sip of the beer. Yu looked very confused and I laughed again as I put the beer down and went to check on dinner.

The pot pies were ready so I grabbed a potholder and pulled the first one out. I walked out to the table, carefully flipped it over onto Yu's plate and removed the aluminum bowl it was in.

I said, "It's very hot, let it cool for a minute."

Then I ran back inside and got the other one and walked back out. As I flipped it on to my plate, I could see that the sun was just starting to touch the treetops on the west side of the lake. I walked over and turned the deck lights on before I sat down. The Jim Croce CD had started over for about the third time. I thought about changing it, but Yu seem to be enjoying it so I left it alone. I poked at the pot pie with my fork. The steam rolled off of it like smoke from a fire. I put a small amount on my fork and blew on it. I was trying to be very animated. Yu seemed to understand and did the same. We ate dinner pretty much in silence. I was at a loss for what to talk about. Yu would be gone tomorrow anyway so I figured this was best. We just listened to the music and ate. It was very nice.

After dinner, I got up and walked into the cabin. Croce was getting old. I put on a Jimmy Buffet CD and walked back out onto the deck. I could see Yu looking up towards the speakers again with a big smile on her face. I assumed that she approved of my choice. The sun was down now and the boats lights lit up the deck. The water shimmered like a flickering candle. I walked back to the table and started picking up the dishes. I could see that Yu's glass was empty, so I asked her, "Can I get you another soda, or something else to drink?

Yu thought for a second and quietly shook her head from side to side.

I asked again, "Did you have enough to eat?"

She shook her head up and down indicating that she had. I picked up the dishes and began to carry them to the sink in the kitchen. Then I returned with another beer. I sat the beer on the table and lit a cigarette. I walked over to the pole rack and took the deep sea fishing pole and reel that my father had given me. I walked back over to the table, opened my beer, sat down, and started setting the pole up for Speckled Trout. When the pole was ready I leaned it up against the table, took a sip of my beer, and walked back into the cabin for some bait. I pulled a box of glow beetles out of the tackle box I kept under the sink.

As I walked back to the table, I couldn't help but notice that Yu was looking first at her empty can of soda and then at my can of beer. It was obvious to her that something was different. I picked up the pole and baited the hook with the beetles. I then stepped to the side of the deck and cast the line out onto the lake and let the bobber float about fifteen feet from the Pearl. I placed the handle of the rod in the pole holder then sat back down and waited for a bite. I crushed out my cigarette in the ashtray and took a sip of my beer.

Yu's curiosity finally got the best of her and she asked as she pointed to the beer, "What?"

I laughed and said, "It's a beer. Would you like to taste it?"

I held the can of beer up and Yu slowly took it and put it to her mouth. The look on her face told the whole story. She obviously did not care for the taste of beer. She quickly handed the can back to me and started looking for somewhere to spit it out.

I started to laugh as I handed her the empty glass she had been using and said, "Spit it in here."

Yu couldn't get the nasty taste of the beer out quick enough. She spit the beer into the glass as politely as she could. Her face was shriveled up like a prune as I set the can of beer back down on the table and walked into the kitchen to bring her back a glass of water. Yu gulped the water down very quickly.

After recovering for a couple of minutes, Yu looked up at me and said very seriously, "Not good."

I just laughed and said, "I like it."

Yu began to smile again and I was still laughing to myself when the fishing pole started popping up and down in the holder. I jumped out of my chair and grabbed the pole. I could tell from the way it pulled that this was a good one. I turned my head and asked Yu to get the net hanging on the wall. She ran over, grabbed the net, and brought it to me. She stood just off to my side as she watched and waited until I needed it. I fought the fish for a good five minutes but finally got it to the surface. It was a very nice size trout. It was a ten, maybe twelve-pounder. I reached over and took the net from Yu and as I held the tip of the pole high, I dipped the net into the water under the fish. I laid the pole down, grabbed the net with both hands, and hoisted the fish up on to the deck. I was very happy. It was one of the nicest trout I had ever caught. Today was turning out to be a great day.

I dragged the net and the fish over to the center of the deck as I had done with the catfish yesterday. The trout was jumping all over the place. I grabbed a small wooden bat hanging on the cabin wall and hit the flopping fish on the head three times. The trout stopped its desperate attempt to get away and there was just a slight twitch every now and then. I was learning. My arm still hurt from yesterday. I pulled the fish out of the net and removed the hook from its mouth. I carried it over to the cleaning table at the front of the deck and placed it in the large stainless steel sink. I backed up to get a good look at it. It was longer than the sink. I turned and ran up to Yu and grabbed her by the shoulders. I danced around her smiling and laughing. She was smiling back and seemed to enjoy the moment as much as I did.

I knew I would need a large freezer bag for that size fish. I ran into the kitchen and started opening drawers and cabinet doors looking for the zip lock bags again. It took a few minutes, but I finally located them and started back out onto the deck. As I walked back outside I couldn't believe what I saw. Yu already had the head off the trout and had gutted it. She was running a knife down the back of its spine and as I watched in amazement she surgically removed both fillets off each side of the huge trout. She then flipped each fillet over and putting the knife between the skin and the meat, slid the knife effortlessly away from herself and removed the skin. I walked over to the counter and looked at what she had done. They were two of the most beautiful fillets of meat I had ever seen. Not one bone and not even the slightest waste of meat. She had done this in just a few minutes. I knew it would have taken me at least thirty minutes and I would've probably butchered the job.

I looked at Yu and smugly said, "Nice job." As if I could have done better.

I finished cutting the filets into four pieces each and slipped them into the zip lock bags.

I thought to myself, "This woman would make some man a great husband."

I finished cleaning up the cleaning table and brought the bags of fish into the kitchen.

As I placed them into the freezer, I turned to Yu and said, "It's been a long day. Are you about ready for bed?"

The smile left Yu's face instantly. She didn't say a word.

I said, "Let's get some sleep and head out for the marina first thing in the morning."

I put my arm around her shoulders and walked her towards the bedroom. Her head dropped forward slightly and her eyes became very sad looking. I thought she probably wanted to stay up and keep the party going. But I was tired and I didn't get a nap like she had. As we entered the bedroom I turned the covers down on the bed and showed Yu how to turn the bed light on and off.

I said, "You know where the bathroom is and if you need anything. Just call out to me. I will be in the loft bed, just outside the door."

Yu's eyes opened wide again and the smile came back. As I walked out the door and closed it behind me, she jumped onto the bed giggling like a small child. I started turning out lights throughout the cabin. I turned the CD player off and climbed the ladder to the loft beds. It had turned out to be a great day and I had no trouble falling asleep.

Chapter 4

It was still dark when I awoke the next morning. I rolled over and looked out the window. The light blue and white line on the horizon let me know that the sun would be up soon. I crawled down the ladder from the loft and started turning the galley lights on. A shower would have been nice, but Yu was still a sleep and I didn't want to wake her. I usually didn't eat breakfast, or do a lot of cooking for myself, but I thought I would make some sausage, eggs, and maybe some pancakes, before the sun came up and we headed north for the marina. I lit a cigarette and began to get the project started, trying to be as quiet as I could. I had no idea how Yu would like her eggs so I decided that I would just scramble them all.

As I set the table and poured a couple of glasses of milk, I looked over and saw the pancake smoking and burning on the griddle. I quickly slid the spatula under it, but it was too late. The pancake was toast. Burnt to a crisp. As I tossed it into the trash can and poured another cake onto the griddle I laughed to myself as I remembered what my father used to tell me as a small child. Pancakes are like kids. You get to throw the first one away. I was still chuckling to myself when I heard the sounds of life coming from the bedroom. A few minutes later the bedroom door opened and a very sleepy looking Yu stepped out. Her hair looked like she was trying out for the lead role in a horror movie. She was barefoot and rubbing both eyes with her fists.

Smiling, I said, "Good morning, Sunshine. Are you hungry?"

Yu lowered her hands and looked up at me. She slowly formed a tiny smile on her face and shook her head up and down. It was starting to get light outside as I put my arm around Yu and led her to the table. She was walking much better now and seemed to be getting stronger. The sun was not up yet, but it wouldn't be long before we could get underway. As Yu sat down at the table, I took her plate and filled it with the sausage, eggs and pancakes. Then I served up my own breakfast and sat down to join her. Yu looked a little skeptical as she picked up her fork and started poking at her food. I quickly realized that she wasn't familiar with what was in front of her.

I had no idea of what she was used to eating back in the Bayous, but it was obvious that this was unusual to her. I stopped what I was doing and reached across the table to put a little butter and syrup on her pancake. I then took the saltshaker and shook a little on her eggs. She watched me very closely as I returned to eating my own breakfast. Yu began to taste the items on her plate. As she did she looked up and smiled at me with what I took as approval. I was in a hurry to get started that morning so I found myself finished with my breakfast well before Yu was done. As I stood up from the table, I said, "I'm going to jump into the shower real quick. Take your time and finish your breakfast. I won't be long." And with that, I walked into the bedroom, closed the door, and started the shower.

When I had finished my shower and put on some clean cloths, I stepped out of the bedroom. Yu had finished her breakfast and was sitting there quietly with her hands folded in her lap. I walked over to the refrigerator and poured her another glass of milk. I began to clear the dishes off the table. I filled the sink with hot water and placed the dishes in it to soak. I looked over at Yu and began to laugh. She was putting her glass back down on the table and had a very large milk mustache. She looked puzzled at my laughter, but said nothing.

After the dishes were in the sink, I went into the bedroom and dug out another pair of sweat pants and a sweatshirt. I only had the two pair and I figured I would lose this one when Yu left this afternoon. I laid them out on the bed with a fresh pair of briefs and another pair of socks. I stepped back into the galley and escorted Yu into the bedroom. I turned the shower on and adjusted the water. I told her that she could shower as I started our trip across the lake. She didn't say anything and I left her standing there as I closed the bedroom door behind me and headed for the helm.

I started the engine and raised the anchors. I pushed the throttle forward and headed the Pearl north. I flipped through my CD case and found a CD that always made me feel-good. A little Sinatra seemed to be in order so I slid Old Blue Eyes into the CD player and turned it up. The sun was up now; the lake was calm, and the sky was blue as I steered the Pearl for the horizon. I knew it would take about two and a half hours to cross the lake so I sat back in my captain's chair and helped Frank "Do It My Way."

Frank and I were in the middle of New York, New York when the bedroom door opened and Yu stepped out. I stopped singing and smiled at her as she walked to the kitchen table and sat down. I was surprised to see that she was actually wearing the socks and slippers. She had the comb in her hand and was making a valiant attempt to use it. I checked my heading and flipped the ring over the steering wheel. I walked to the bathroom and brought back the hair dryer. I took her hand and had her change seats so that I was facing the front of the cabin. That way I could keep an eye on the lake in front of us as the Pearl cruised along on autopilot. I plugged in the hair dryer, took the comb, and started drying her hair. She got into it immediately. She laid her head back, closed her eyes, and listened to the music. The smile that was now becoming a more frequent occurrence was plastered on her face. I laughed and realized she could get used to this. After her hair was dried, I took the comb and hair dryer back to the bathroom.

As I walked back I asked Yu, "Would you like a Pepsi®?"

Yu smiled again and shook her head up and down. As I took two of the drinks out of the refrigerator, I made a mental note to put some more in later. I opened one of the cans and handed it to her. Then I sat back down in the captain's chair, flipped the ring off of the steering wheel, opened my drink, and continued our trip across the lake. Frank was still filling the room with his music while Yu was tapped her feet and swayed her head back and forth in time.

We had been traveling for about an hour when the CD reached its last song. Yu had been sitting there quietly listening, sipping on her soda, and not saying anything. I wondered to myself if she was worried about what would happen when we reached the marina. Come to think of it, I wondered if she even had any idea what was going to happen. I hadn't given it much thought until now, but I realized that even I didn't know what would happen to her. After I reported the guy laying back there dead, and that I couldn't have just left her there, I was sure that whoever the responsible party was would take her and help her get back on her feet. I knew that was what had to happen, but I prayed it would not be another traumatic experience for her. I sat there sipping my drink and tried not to think about it.

The last song ended and Yu looked at me as if to say, "What's next?"

I was getting tired of the CD player, but we had another hour or so to go before we got to the north shore. I decided that maybe Yu would like to watch some television so I took the remote control and clicked on the satellite dish. I had a forty-two inch flat screen TV that was mounted on the front cabin wall. I used it for both my computer monitor and a television set. As it came on I flipped it over to CNN to see what was happening in the world. Yu's mouth dropped as she stared at the screen. Wolf was talking about the war efforts in Iraq. I quickly realized that Yu had never seen a television program. All the things that I took for granted were a huge surprise to her. I realized that she would not understand things like the news and what was happening in a world that she didn't even know existed. I clicked on the menu and found a Shirley Temple movie that was just starting. Yu didn't say a thing; she just stared at the screen in amazement.

As Yu watched the movie, the hour slipped by quickly. I could see the north shoreline ahead. It would only be another fifteen or twenty minutes before we reached it. I was hoping that it wouldn't be too hard to find the marina. Yu was still engrossed in the movie. She was smiling from ear to ear so I knew she was enjoying it. As we got closer to the north side of the lake I could see a flag and some buildings. I figured that it must be the marina so I adjusted my course and headed for it. As we got closer, I could see that it was the marina and a fairly large one at that. There were four sets of docks. There were a few very nice boats moored to a couple of them. One of the docks had gas pumps so I headed for it.

As we pulled closer I killed the engine and drifted towards the gas pumps. A young man ran out to grab the front of the Pearl and help guide it in. I stepped out onto the front deck and tossed the young man the mooring line. The young man grabbed it and started to pull the nose of the Pearl towards the tide down. I walked back through the bedroom and opened the back door. I stepped out on to the rear deck, took the other mooring line, and jumped on to the dock. I pulled the back of the Pearl to the dock and tied her off.

As the young man approached I said, "Fill her up with fuel and where can I get water and dump my sewage tanks?"

The young man replied, "We can handle it all right here." He continued, "We have fresh water and a sewage pump."

I asked him, "Is there a police or ranger station located here?"

He very politely responded, "No sir, but they can contact them for you up at the store."

I thanked him for his help and jumped back onto the Pearl. As I walked back into the living room, Yu was still enthralled with her movie. I picked up the remote and hit pause.

Yu snapped her head around and looked up at me as if to say, "What happened?"

I smiled at her and said, "I have to go up to the store for a little while, but I will not be gone for long. Stay on the boat and watch your movie. I will be back as soon as I can."

Yu said, "Ok," as she turned back towards the TV.

I pushed the play button on the remote. Shirley and Bo Jangles started dancing again. Yu's head tilted back and forth as she watched and listened to the music.

The young man was working on the Pearl as I stepped onto the dock and headed up to the store. The dock was a very wide wooden dock with a nonskid coating of some kind. The marina appeared to be in very good upkeep. As I approached the store, I saw a street and other buildings that ran along behind it. It was a quaint little town nestled in a large group of cypress trees. It was very pretty and smelled of springtime. I thought to myself maybe they have a Laundromat here. I could sure use one. I walked into the store and a small cowbell rang against the door.

There was a heavyset woman behind the counter that looked up at me as I entered and said, "Morning."

I nodded my head and walked over to where she was. She was a nice looking woman and had a very pretty smile. She was dressed very nicely, but was wearing way too much perfume.

I said, "Good morning, can you tell me how to get in touch with the rangers station or the police department?"

She looked at me with a big smile on her face and said, "Why? Did someone die, Sweetie?"

I said, "Yes ma'am."

Her face went white and the smile disappeared. She said, "You're kidding?"

I said, "No ma'am," and I told her about Yu and the man in the shack.

She became very serious and told me to hold on a second as she walked over to the radio and turned it on. She keyed the mike and said, "Ranger One, this is the North Side Marina, do you copy?"

A second later I could hear a voice on the speaker say, "Yeah Alice, this is Ranger One, we copy."

Alice keyed the mike again and said, "Roy, you had better get over here quick. I have a guy here that found a dead body."

Roy came back and said, "Well, it will be about an hour before we can get there. We're on the east side of the lake. Can he stick around?"

Alice looked over at me with that question in her eyes.

I quickly answered, "Sure, that's not a problem."

Alice keyed the mike again and said, "Yeah, he'll wait for you Roy."

Roy came back with, "OK, we'll be there as soon as we can. Ranger one out."

I gave Alice my name and told her I would be on The Black Pearl down by the fuel pumps.

Alice said, "That will be fine, Sweetie."

I thanked her and headed back towards the dock. I knew I needed a few supplies, but they could wait until this was all done.

I hadn't been gone a long time, but as I reached the Pearl the young man had finished fueling the boat and pumping the sewage.

He walked up to me and said, "Full of fuel and water, and the sewage has all been pumped out."

I thanked him and gave him my credit card. The young man was gone for a moment and then came back with my receipt. I signed for the services and thanked him again. As I hopped back up on the Pearl, I could hear Yu crying from inside. I rushed in to the cabin to see what was wrong.

Yu looked up at me with tears streaming down her cheeks and pointed at the TV. She said, "Puppy hurt!"

I pulled a handkerchief out of my back pocket and handed it to her as I kneeled down beside her chair.

I said, "Yu, it's only a movie. It's not a real."

Yu looked up at me with tears still welling up in her eyes and said, "Yes, I saw."

I felt horrible. Her heart was really breaking. I took Yu's hand and quietly said, "Yu, a movie is just a story. The people and the dog in the movie are just actors. They pretend to be people you see in the story." I continued, "The puppy is not really hurt. They just make it look like he is, because it's part of the story."

Yu looked up at me and asked, "Puppy not hurt?"

I smiled and replied, "That's the truth. They make all kinds of movies. Scary ones, funny ones, and some that make you sad." I continued, "You just keep watching this and I will bet that Shirley gets her dog back, and that the story ends with her being really happy. All her movies do."

Yu was crying a little softer now. I took the handkerchief and wiped her cheeks.

I told her, "You just keep watching and I bet you will be smiling in just a few minutes."

I pulled a chair up next to hers and held her hand. We watched the movie together and within five minutes Shirley Temple had her dog back and all was right with the world again.

After the movie was over I asked, "Would you like to watch another movie?"

Yu looked up at me and asked, "Sleep?"

I realized that she was exhausted. The movie had taken a lot out of her. It was obvious that she was still weak and became tired very easily. I helped her up and walked her to the bedroom.

She crawled upon the bed and I took her slippers off. I pulled the bedspread up over her and closed the bedroom door as I walked back into the living room. I turned the channel over to CNN and watched the news while I waited on the rangers.

It was almost two hours before the rangers showed up. As they came aboard, I met them at the sliding glass doors and asked them if we could talk on the dock. Yu was still asleep, but I wanted to talk to them away from her. I grabbed the piece of paper that I had written the GPS coordinates on back at the shack as I walked out the door and closed it behind me.

As they stepped onto the dock, the larger of the two rangers stuck out his hand and said, "I'm Roy and this is Jerry."

I shook Roy's hand and said to him, "I'm Terry glad to meet you." I told Roy and Jerry how I had gotten lost in the bayous and how I had happened upon the shack. I told them how I had found the guy dead on the bed, about Yu, the condition she was in, and about the rope that was on her leg. I told them how hungry and thirsty she had been and why I felt that I couldn't just leave her there alone. I gave the rangers the paper with the GPS coordinates on it. And waited for their response.

Roy thanked me for my report and assured me that he would send someone out to retrieve the body and file a report.

The two rangers started to turn and walk away, when I said, "Just a minute, what about the girl?"

The rangers turned back around and Roy asked, "What about the girl?"

I asked, "Aren't you going to take her somewhere, where she can get some help?"

Roy asked, "Is she hurt?"

I said, "No, not that I can tell."

Roy responded, "We have no reason to take the girl. We don't have the authority or the resources for that kind of thing."

I asked, "Then what do I do with her?"

Roy thought for a moment, and then said, "You might try the police department in New Orleans. If they can't help you, they may know of an organization that can."

There was a long pause. Finally, I said, "I understand. I'll try the police in New Orleans."

Roy shook my hand and said, "Good luck." Then he and Jerry turned and walked away.

As I walked back into the cabin, Yu was just coming out of the bedroom. I reached into the refrigerator grabbed the last Pepsi® and a beer. I opened the can and motioned Yu to sit down. She was still rubbing her eyes as she took the soda and sat down at the kitchen table. I opened my beer and sat in the captain's chair across from her. I picked up the remote and turned off the TV. It was clear to me that Yu would be with me a couple more days. That concerned me. I really didn't want her to become too attached to the Pearl or me. I was worried it might be hard enough for her to leave as it was, and she had only been here for less than twenty-four hours. As different as it had to be for her, she appeared to have enjoyed herself while she was here. I was just afraid two more days might make it even harder on both of us. I sipped at my beer and lit a cigarette.

I looked over at Yu and asked, "Did you have a nice nap?"

She smiled back and shook her head up and down. It was just a little past noon. I needed a few supplies from the store. I thought it might be nice for Yu to get off the boat for a little while if she thought she had the strength.

I asked her, "Would you like to go up to the store with me and get some more Pepsi®?"

Her eyes widened and she shook her head up and down.

I smiled and said, "Ok, we'll go after we finish our drinks."

As Yu and I stepped onto the dock, the young man that had filled up the Pearl earlier walked up to us. As he did, Yu grabbed my arm, got real close to me, and lowered her head. The boy stopped his approach and dropped his smile. He looked confused, like maybe he had done something wrong.

I touched Yu's hand and said, "It's okay. This is the nice man that put gas in the boat."

She looked up at me but said nothing.

I turned to the young man and asked, "Can I do something for you?"

He hesitated for a second then said, "Can we move your boat down a little, in case someone else needs fuel?"

I smiled at him and said, "Sure. Can you get the back line?"

He nodded affirmatively and headed for the rear of the Pearl. I asked Yu to follow me as I untied the front mooring line. The young man and I had no trouble pulling the Pearl down the dock and retied her off when the fuel pumps had been cleared enough.

The young man yelled, "Thanks."

I waved and took Yu's hand and we started up the docks toward the store.

As Yu and I walked into the store, Alice looked up from behind the counter and said, "Hi Terry and how are you doing, Sugar?"

I'm sure that Yu had no idea that Alice was referring to her, but when Yu saw Alice her face lit up and she smiled like Alice was a long lost friend she hadn't seen in years.

I looked at Alice and said, "We just thought we would pick up a few things for the boat."

She smiled real big and said, "You just knock your self out, Sweetie."

Yu let go of my hand and, still smiling, stared at all the stuff in the store. She looked like a child at Christmas. Yu started slowly walking down the first isle looking at everything.

I started to say something when Alice waved at me and said, "Its OK, Sweetie, just let her look around all she wants."

It was obvious that Roy had told her of our conversation. I smiled at her, as if to say thank you, and she nodded her head back at me. I busied myself picking out the supplies I needed, looking up to check on Yu every few minutes. As I carried the items up to the counter, I did notice that Yu didn't touch anything, but looked at everything. Yu seemed to be amazed at all the stuff as she walked up and down the rows of the small store. After I had gathered all we needed Alice started ringing the items up on the cash register. As I waited for the total I saw Yu standing at a rack of stuffed animals against the wall. I excused myself to Alice and walked over to where Yu was standing. She was looking at a small white teddy bear on the display.

I asked her, "Do you like it?"

Yu looked at me and said, "Pretty."

I picked the bear up and handed it to her. She looked at me with big, open eyes and squeezed it to her chest.

I said, "It's yours. You can keep it."

Yu, looked down at the bear in her hands then back at me and asked, "Mine?"

I said, "Yes, it's yours."

Yu couldn't stand still. She looked over at Alice and walked towards her, holding up the bear to show her and said, "Mine!"

Alice just smiled and said, "You sure have a pretty teddy bear, Sugar."

I walked up to the counter as Yu was squeezing and hugging the stuffed bear, handed Alice my credit card, and said, "Thank you."

Alice just smiled while she ran my card. I quickly stuck out my hand before she did and asked her, "How much do I owe you for mooring?"

Alice looked out the window, then back at me and said, "Shoot, Honey, your not bothering anything where you are. Stay as long as you need, there's no charge."

As Yu and I started to leave the store I stopped and turned back towards Alice and asked, "Is there a Laundromat anywhere close by?"

Alice said, "Sure is, Sweetie, just down the street next to the café."

I thanked her again and we headed back to the Pearl with all our groceries. As I put the groceries away and stocked the fridge with Pepsi®, Yu was dancing around the living room. She was humming and holding her bear, first hugging it close to her chest, then at arms length to smile at it, then back to her chest again. I couldn't quite make out the tune, but I was happy for her. After all the supplies were put away, I went to the linen closet and grabbed a pillowcase. I emptied all the dirty clothes from the hamper into it. I then picked up the few that were lying on the bedroom and bathroom floor and added them to the pile. Yu had done so well at the store I thought we might try another trip out and go to the Laundromat. It was almost one so I thought that if it were next to a café we might get a bite to eat while we were there. I stopped Yu from dancing for a moment and explained what I wanted to do.

She looked at me, smiled, and simply said, "Okay."

Yu and I walked up the long dock and down the sidewalk of the small town hand in hand. As we walked along we approached an older gentleman sitting on a bench outside the barbershop reading the paper. When Yu saw the man she dropped her smile and slid from my right side behind me to my left and held my arm tightly with her head looking down at the sidewalk. I smiled at the gentleman as we past and he looked up and smiled back. Yu didn't smile or look at him and wouldn't let go of my arm. We found the Laundromat without any trouble and walked in. There was a young lady folding clothes on one of the tables. She looked up at us as we came in and smiled.

Yu let go of my arm, smiled back, and said, "Hi!"

The girl responded and said, "Hi," back as she kept on folding cloths.

It was becoming apparent to me that Yu seemed to be afraid of men, but not women. I wondered why she didn't seem to have that fear of me. Was she so hungry and thirsty when I first found her that she had to trust me? Or was it because I took the rope off her leg? Yu stuck close and followed me around the Laundromat like a little puppy. I knew right then that whoever I found in New Orleans, to get her the help she needed, it would have to be a woman. I put the clothes into the washing machines, dumped in the soap, and got them started. Once the washing machines were all running, I took Yu next door to the café while we waited on the clothes to wash. As we opened the café door and stepped inside, I could see the place was empty.

The waitress looked up from where she was sitting, put down her newspaper, and said, "Just have a seat anywhere."

As we sat down at a small booth near the back, the waitress walked up with a couple of menus. I waved off the menus and said, "May we just have two hamburgers, two orders of fries and two Pepsis® please?"

The waitress smiled and said, "Sure, but we don't have Pepsi®, is Coke® all right?"

Yu snapped her head around and stared at the waitress. She looked heart broken. I started to laugh and said, "Coke® is just fine, thank you."

Yu looked at me like I had just betrayed her. I smiled at Yu and said, "Coke® and Pepsi® are the same kind of drink. They just have different names."

Yu looked confused and didn't know what to think. The waitress came back with the two glasses of Coke® and set them down on the table. She said, "The burgers will be up in just a minute."

I said, "Thanks." and she walked away. I looked at Yu and said, "Try it."

Yu picked up the glass, took a sip and slowly smiled. I laughed. Yu was cute and funny. Yu and I sat there without saying much of anything, just smiling and drinking our sodas. A few minutes later the waitress came back with our order and placed them on the table.

The waitress looked at me and said, "Can I get you and your daughter anything else?" I hadn't thought of it before, but all of a sudden I felt very old. I looked up at the waitress smiling and said, "No, thank you, this is fine."

Yu picked up her fork and looked somewhat puzzled. I could tell she didn't know how to attack the hamburger. I picked mine up and held it so that she could see to use her hands. I took a bite and placed it back down on my plate. Yu smiled and did the same. I then poured a little ketchup on my plate then hers and dipped one of my French-fries into it and took a bite. She followed my lead. We sat there and laughed and ate our lunch without saying a word.

It had been about thirty minutes since we had come in the café. I was finished with my lunch and Yu just had a little more to eat. I called the waitress over and ordered an ice cream sundae for Yu. I waited until she brought it over before I explained to Yu that I needed to go put the clothes in the dryer. Yu picked up her fork and took a bite of the sundae. Her eyes got real big and she said, "Good. I like."

I laughed and said, "Ok, you sit here and eat your ice cream and I will be back in a minute or two."

Yu didn't even look up as she said, "Ok."

I wasn't gone for more than five minutes. I took the wet clothes out of the washing machines and put them in the dryer. I had to use five quarters to get the dryer to last an hour. When I came back into the café, Yu was scrapping the bottom of the Sunday dish with her fork. I walked over to the table and picked up her spoon and handed it to her.

Smiling, I said, "Here try this."

She looked up at me, then looked at the spoon and took it from my hand. She studied it for a second then scooped up the melted ice cream in the bottom of her dish. She looked up and smiled at me as she put the spoon in her mouth. We had an hour before the clothes would be dry. So I decided that we would take a walk and see what there was to see in this small little backwoods town. I walked over to the waitress and paid the bill. As I walked back to the table, I dropped three dollars on it, reached out my hand, and asked Yu if she was ready. Yu looked up at me smiling, took my hand, and crawled out of the booth. As we walked towards the door, I thanked the waitress again and Yu turned her head towards the young lady and said, "Bye."

The waitress was clearing the table as she looked back at us and said, "You guys come back now."

As we walked out of the small café I saw a park across the street next to a building that said City Hall on it. There was no traffic at all on the street of this sleepy little town, but I looked both ways before we started across. My mother would be proud of me. As we came to the grassy little park I saw an old fashion merry-go-round. The kind we had in the schoolyard in elementary school.

I lead Yu over to it and helped her step up as I said, "Hold on to the bar."

I took the bar that she was holding onto, slowly started walking, and turning the merry-go-round in a clockwise direction. As I felt Yu was getting more comfortable with what I was doing I increased my walk to a jog. Yu started smiling so I increased the pace a little faster. She started laughing and held on tighter to the bar. I started running, pushing the merry-go-round as fast as I could then jumped on next to her. Yu was screaming and laughing at the same time. We road around together for a little over a minute until it came to a stop. Yu was laughing and having a good time. When it finally did stop she looked at me and asked, "Again?"

I was still huffing and puffing from the first time. I thought to myself I was definitely smoking too much. I made a mental note to cut down on the cigarettes. I stepped back down and got the merry-go-round going again. Yu's screams and laughter was infectious. I found myself laughing and feeling like a kid again. But I was far from being a kid and when we came to a stop the second time and Yu said, "Again?"

I said, "No, no, no."

I would probably have a heart attack if I did. I took Yu over to the swing set and sat her in the seat. I then very slowly pulled her back a little and told her to raise her feet. I let go and as she swung away, then back, I pushed her just a little harder. She got the idea quickly and before long I was pushing her to a pretty good height. She held onto the small chains that attached to the seat and laughed and screamed each time I pushed her a little higher. Yu was having fun and I was able to rest and catch my breath from the merry-go-round. It was perfect for both of us.

We stayed in the park for the full hour. After the swings I showed her how to use the monkey bars and then we seesawed. Before we left, however, we had to do the merry-go-round one more time. Folding clothes never appealed to me more than it did right then. When the hour had past we walked back across the street and entered the Laundromat. I pulled the clothes from the dryer and put them on a table. Yu watched me very closely as I folded the clothes and put them in the pillowcase. Once I was finished, I swung the pillowcase over my shoulder and we started back towards the Pearl. Yu held my free hand and was almost skipping as we walked along. I could tell she was getting much better. Her strength was returning and she was looking much healthier.

Once back onboard, I laid the pillowcase full of the clean clothes on the bed. It was a little after three and, even though I knew we could not reach New Orleans before nightfall, I decided that we could at least get to the channel that lead to the canal and spend the night there. I walked back into the living room and turned on the TV. I found two movies that were just about to start. *Old Yeller* and *Mary Poppins*. I laughed to myself knowing that there was no way in hell I was going to let Yu watch *Old Yeller*. I could just imagine the screaming that would occur when they shot the dog. I flipped the channel over to *Mary Poppins* and told Yu that, after I put the clothes away, I had to run up to the store for just a second. She settled in to watch the movie and nodded her head as if to say ok. I walked back into the bedroom and put the clothes into their respective drawers. As I walked past Yu she was already engrossed in the show.

I said, "I'll be back in a minute" and I walked out the door.

As I entered the store Alice was stocking shelves. She looked up and said, "Hi Sweetie, did you find the Laundromat?"

I said, "I sure did, thank you." As I walked over to where Alice was working, I asked, "Sweet Heart, how far is the channel that takes you up to the canal from here?"

"About ten or eleven miles," She answered. She got up from what she was doing and took me over to a map hanging on the wall. As she pointed to the map she said, "Here's where we are; and here's the channel."

I asked, "Do you have an atlas of the U.S that has GPS coordinates on it?"

She walked over behind the counter and started shuffling around in the cabinet. "Got one left," She announced as she brought it up and laid it on the counter top. "Just twenty-four, ninety-five," She added. I pulled out my wallet and handed her my credit card. "Are you going to be staying here tonight," She asked?

I answered, "No ma'am, I'm going to head down to the channel and spend the night there. That way I can get an early start tomorrow for New Orleans."

Alice handed me back my card and said, "Well you just take good care of that little girl, you hear! She's a sweetie-pie."

"I'm doing my best," I answered. "And you're right, she is a sweet heart." I picked up the atlas, thought to myself, one down two to go, thanked Alice once more for all her help, and headed back to the Pearl.

I walked into the cabin with the sound of "A spoon full of sugar" softly coming from the TV. Yu was still sitting there, clutching her teddy bear, and swaying to the music. She looked up at me with a big smile and said, "Hi!"

I laid the atlas down and asked, "Is it a good movie?"

Yu looked up at me again and said, "I like."

"Well you just enjoy it, I'm going to get the boat ready to shove off," I said. I looked at my watch. It was three thirty-five. I walked out and jumped onto the dock then untied the rear mooring line. I gave the Pearl a little shove to get her back end away from the dock. I then went and untied the front. I jumped back onto the deck and walked into the cabin. I started the engine and backed the Pearl out into open water. I throttled forward and headed east towards the channel.

We got to the channel a little after five. I kept the Pearl off shore about a half mile and stopped the engine. When she had come to a complete stop, I dropped the anchors. Yu's movie was ending so I took the remote and turned the TV off. I took out an instrumental CD and put it on. I opened the fridge and took out a soda and a beer. I reached over and took Yu's hand, lead her out onto the front deck, and sat her at the table. I opened her drink and set it in front of her. I went back into the cabin and got my cigarettes. As I walked back out on the deck, Yu was pretending to give the teddy bear a drink of her soda. I sat down and opened my beer. Yu was smiling and playing with the bear. I started to light a cigarette, then remembered the merry-go-round. I slid the cigarette back into the pack, laid them down on the table, and took a sip of my beer instead. I had decided that I needed to talk to Yu and find out as much as I could about her life back at the shack. That way I could tell who ever was going to take her what kind of life she had been living so they could figure out the best way of helping her.

I touched Yu's hand and asked, "Yu, who was the man back at the shack?"

Yu stopped playing with the bear, thought for a second and said, "Don't know." She turned her attention back to the bear.

I asked, "What was his name?"

Yu stopped, looked over at me, and said, "Sir."

She started to go back playing with the bear, so I took it and placed it on the table where she could still see it and said, "Yu let the pretty teddy bear rest for a minute and lets you and I talk."

She looked at me, then at the bear to make sure it was all right, and then looked back at me and said, "Ok."

I said, "Sir is not a name. It's just what you say when you're being polite. Did he have a name like John, or Bob?"

She thought for a second and said, "No, no name. Sir his name."

I was really confused now. I asked, "How old are you?"

Yu looked at me like she didn't understand the question, then she said, "Don't know."

I asked, "How long did you live there?"

Yu looked up at me and said, "Always."

I asked, "Were you born there?"

Yu thought again and said, "Don't know."

I asked, "Was there ever another woman at the shack?"

Yu's eyes saddened for a second then she said, "No."

I asked, "Was it just you and he there?"

She said, "Yes, just Sir and Yu."

All at once I had a feeling that I knew the answer to my next question but I asked, "Is Yu your real name?"

She paused and thought for a long time then said, "That's what Sir called me when he wanted something."

I realized then that he was saying YOU, not Yu as in a name. I could hear the bastard now. "You get over here. You get those fish cleaned." Without realizing it, I had been doing the same thing. I handed her back the bear and drank my beer. I didn't know what to think.

    I couldn't help caring for Yu, or who ever she was. She was cute, young and definitely deserved a better hand than she had been dealt. I didn't know her history, but I was starting to understand that she got a very raw deal. Today I found out more than I really wanted to know. I had no idea how to help her. Maybe someone in New Orleans could. We spent the rest of the evening pretty much in silence. I made us dinner and we watched some TV together. About nine o'clock I turned out the lights and helped her into bed. I crawled up into the loft and, as I laid my head on the pillow, I prayed for the first time in a long time. It was short, but from the heart. "Please, Lord, watch over her. Let things workout and let her be happy."

Chapter 5

As I climbed down the ladder from the loft the next morning, it was already starting to get light. I looked at my watch as I picked it up off the kitchen counter top. It was five-thirty. I slipped it on my arm and headed for the helm. I started the engine, raised the anchors, and headed for the channel. The trip up the channel, to the canal, took only five or six minutes. It was less than a mile. I laughed at myself thinking about all the miles of channels I had traveled trying to find the lake. As I entered the canal, I made my turn and headed west. With any luck I would be back in New Orleans by five or five-thirty.

The Pearl had been cruising down the canal for about thirty minutes when I thought I heard the shower come on. Because of the hum from the engine I couldn't be sure. About ten minutes later I heard it shut off. Now I was sure that it had been running. About five minutes later I heard the hairdryer going. It was definitely coming from the bathroom. I kept heading west and wondered what was going on in there. A few minutes later the hairdryer stopped. A couple more minutes went by, then the bedroom door opened and Yu stepped out caring her teddy bear. She was all showered, her hair was washed and dried, and wearing the same sweatpants outfit that she had on the day before. I was impressed. I looked back at her and said, "Good morning Miss Sunshine."

She smiled at me and said, "Hi!"

The Rope

I flipped the ring over the steering wheel, reached up into the cabinet, and took down a bowl. I sat it on the table and took out the cornflakes. I poured the cornflakes, added some sugar, and got a banana and some milk from the fridge. I cut the banana up over the bowl of cornflakes then added the milk. I got a spoon from the drawer and set it down next to the bowl. I went back and took the ring off the wheel and told Yu to have a seat and eat some breakfast. She smiled, sat down and began to investigate what was in front of her. After a few seconds of poking around in the bowl she took a bite. She flashed a big smile and started eating.

After Yu was finished with her cereal, she sat there looking at me for a moment then stood up and took her bowl to the sink. She took it, and the few other dishes that were in the sink, out and placed them on the counter top. She then turned on the water to the sink. She stood there and watched as the water emptied out the drain. She looked around for a second and then put the stopper in the sink. After she figured she had enough water she turned it off. She took her bowl, placed it in the water and started rubbing it with her hands. I checked my course and flipped the ring over the wheel. I walked up behind Yu and reach down under the sink to pull out the dish soap. I squeezed a little into the sink and ran my hand through the water rapidly to make some suds. I then reached up and took a sponge and wiped the bowl with it. I held the bowl over the other sink, turned the water back on, and rinsed it off. I placed the clean bowl into the strainer to let it dry. She looked at me, smiling with approval, and I walked back over to the wheel.

Yu washed the other dishes, rinsed them off, and put them in the strainer. She pulled the plug and drained the sink. She then ran some more water, wiped the suds out, and cleaned both the sinks. As she sat back at the table, she looked up at me and gave me another smile.

I returned her smile and said, "Thank you. You did a very nice job." I took out the Jimmy Buffet CD and put it on. I looked at Yu and said, "There's soft drink in the refrigerator."

Yu stood up and walked to the refrigerator. She opened the fridge and took out a can of soda. As she walked back to her seat, she looked at the top of the can for a moment then handed it to me. I laughed and holding the top so she could see it, I pulled the tab and opened it for her. She took the can and paused for a moment, then said very quietly, "Thank you." She sat back down, sipping her drink, and listened to the music.

We had only been on the canal for two hours when we reached the channel that I had taken the night I had gotten lost. I knew it was about twenty miles from the channel that lead off the lake. We should still be about thirty minutes away. I suddenly realized that we were traveling with the current again and making better time than I had predicted. I thought to myself, maybe we will get to New Orleans sooner than I had thought. That would help a lot.

Yu was sitting at the table quietly listening to the music, staring out the sliding glass doors at the canal in front of us. There were no other boats on the canal. She had impressed the hell out of me this morning so I slid the captain's chair back as far as it would go and I reached over and took her hand. I pulled her up and guided her over in front of me. Still sitting on the chair, I reached around her and placed her hands on the wheel. I said, "Why don't you drive for a while." Yu turned her head towards me, looking like she didn't understand. I said, "Watch where you're going" and she turned back around and stared out the window.

I took her hands and rolled the wheel to the left so she could see the boat turn. Then I rolled the wheel back to the right and she smiled as we headed back the other way. I took my hands away from hers; I pointed to the left, and said, "Turn left." She rolled the wheel left and laughed as the boat headed in that direction. I then said, "Ok turn it back to where we were." She rolled the wheel right and, still laughing, watched as the boat headed where she had wanted it to go. I sat back in the chair and let her drive the Pearl from one side of the canal to the other and back. It was obvious that she was having a good time.

After a few minutes of weaving down the canal and fearing I might get sea sick, I said, "Ok, now take her back to the right side and go straight down the canal." Yu rolled the wheel to the right then, as she approached the concrete levy wall on the right side, she turned the wheel left until she was headed straight down the canal. I was impressed again.

Once she had the Pearl heading straight down the canal, she turned her head around and looked at me smiling from ear to ear. I laughed and said again, "Watch where you're going" and she snapped her head back around to look out the window once more. I leaned forward and took the throttle in my hand. She watched my every move. I pushed the throttle forward and the Pearl picked up speed. I said, "Fast." Then I slowly pulled the throttle back and the Pearl started slowing down. I said, "Slow." Then I pushed it back to where I had it originally and took my hand away. I said, "Ok, lets go faster." Yu hesitated for a moment, glanced back at me, and then back out the window. She took the throttle in her hand and pushed it forward. The Pearl sped up. Yu started smiling and laughing at her achievement. Then I said, "Lets go slower now." There was no hesitation. Yu pulled back on the throttle and the Pearl slowed down. I said, "Lets go even slower." So Yu pulled the throttle all the way back and the Pearl started coming to a stop. I laughed and said, "Not that slow, speed her up just a little." Yu pushed the throttle forward just a smidge and the Pearl crawled forward. Yu turned and looked at me smiling big time. I smiled back and said, "Ok, lets go back to the speed we were at when we started." Yu thought for a moment then pushed the throttle forward to almost the exact spot it was in at the beginning. The Pearl cruised down the canal just as before.

I slid out of the chair and pushed it forward as far as it would go. Then I held the wheel as I helped Yu up so she could sit down. She re-took the wheel with both hands and smiled like a Cheshire cat as she piloted the Pearl down the canal. I walked over to the fridge and got a soda. I walked back up to the kitchen table and took a seat. Yu looked over at me still smiling. I looked at her, smiled, and said, "You're the captain now. You drive for a while." She smiled again and turned back to peer out the window. I sat back and sipped the soda, but watched her and the canal very closely.

The canal was straight. No turns at all. Normally it would be an extremely boring ride. But Yu was having a ball and I couldn't help enjoying myself watching her. When lunch came around, I made a couple of ham sandwiches. I handed her one and laughed as she held it in one hand as she ate and kept the other hand on the wheel, never taking her eyes off the canal. She was becoming a pro at this. I laughed to myself and thought about re-naming her Tug Boat Annie. I changed the CDs a couple of times over the next few hours, but Yu never gave any impression she wanted to relinquish her duties as captain back to me.

It was about four o'clock as we came into the outskirts of the city and the canal made its turn towards the south. Yu had done a wonderful job. She didn't seem to appreciate it when I took her hand and helped her down off the captain's chair so I could take over. The river was just a mile or so ahead. We had made excellent time. There was very little traffic on the river as I made my turn northwards. It was only about five miles to the docks where I had moored five days ago. We were going against the current of the Mississippi now and it took a good forty minutes to get there. As I pulled into the dock, I was elated that we were there an hour earlier than I had thought we would be.

The Rope

Yu had come out on the deck and watched as the dockhand and I got the Pearl tied off and secured for the night. I yelled over to the young man that I would be there in a few minutes to settle up with him.

He yelled back, "Take your time. I'll be here all night."

I walked Yu back into the cabin and sat her at the kitchen table. I figured I would put a movie on to keep her occupied as I settled up with the dockhand and found out where the Police station was. I turned on the TV and hit menu.

As the menu appeared, Yu pointed towards the screen and said, "Mary Poppins."

I looked at the menu and sure enough Mary Poppins was coming on again. I looked at Yu then back to the screen. I wondered to my-self: if she had read that or just wanted to see it again? I looked at Yu and said, "What does the line below Mary Poppins say?"

Yu looked for a second then said, "Small…soldiers."

I said, "How about the line below that?"

She looked again and said, "King…Kong."

She was correct. She was reading. I looked at Yu and asked, "Where did you learn how to read?"

She looked up at me; as if she might be in trouble then said, "Don't know."

I said, "It's ok; I'm glad that you know how to read. Did he teach you how?"

She looked a little more at ease and said, "No."

I asked, "Did you read books or anything at the shack?"

She thought for a second and said, "No."

My confusion was over shadowed by the mystery of it all. I clicked on Mary Poppins. It had already started. I told Yu that I had to leave for a while but to watch the movie, stay on the boat, and I would be back soon.

As I started to leave, I took the keys out of the helm console. I didn't want Tug Boat Annie taking the Pearl on a joy ride. I stepped onto the dock and walked to the pump shack. I handed the young man my credit card and told him I would be staying through tomorrow night. I asked him where the Police station was.

As he ran my card, he said, "There's a police sub-station two blocks down and one block over to the right."

I took my card, signed the receipt, and said, "Thank you." I walked up the dock and down the two blocks he had told me about. I turned right and headed down the street. The sub-station was easy to find with all the police cars and officers in front of it. The Winchell's doughnut shop across the street was busy. I walked up the steps and entered the building.

As I walked up to the counter a young female officer sitting at a desk, stood up and said, "Good afternoon, can I help you with something?"

I replied, "Yes ma'am, I was told by the Rangers over on Lake Borgne, that you might be able to help me with a small situation I have." I started to explain how I had found the dead guy in the Bayous and how I had brought Yu back with me. I continued, "They said you might be able to take the young lady, or tell me who I could talk too that would."

The lady officer listened to my story, then picked up the phone and dialed. I heard her say, "Detective Rogers, would you come up to the front desk, please." She hung up and said to me, "Detective Rogers would be the best person to help you with this. He will be up here in a moment."

A few minutes later the door opened. A familiar looking gentleman in a suit and tie stepped out. It took a second but as I approached him and extended my arm I said, "Charlie!" He was with Frank in the bar last week. He was the one that told me about Lake Borgne. He had never mentioned he was a cop.

He took my hand and as we shook he finally recognized me and said, "Terry, how are you? Did you make it over to the lake?"

I smiled and said, "Yeah, that's why I'm here." I began to tell Charlie all about the trip and how I became involved with Yu. I told him that I was looking for someone or some organization that could take her and get her the help she needed.

Charlie rubbed his chin, thought for a second, and said, "That might be complicated." Charlie continued, "Come on back to my desk and lets see what we can find."

As we reached Charlie's desk I took a seat and watched as Charlie flipped through a large binder that was lying on his desktop. He studied it for a few minutes then picked up his phone and dialed. I heard him say, "Hey, George, this is Charlie over at Precinct Three. Do you know if the Sisters of Hope complex has opened up again?" There was a long pause as he listened. Then he said, "Do you know of any other faith based or non-faith based organizations like that, that are open?" There was another long pause then Charlie said, "Ok, thanks George. Say hi to Cindy for me." Then he placed the receiver back on its cradle.

Charlie thumbed through the binder for a few more minutes, then looked up at me and said, "The Sisters of Hope complex was a gated community just east of town that took in almost anyone. They provided housing, schooling and medical, almost anything that you needed. They would find you work or your lost family. They were great, but hurricane Katrina wiped them out. According to George they probably won't be re-building. They just don't have the resources or support they had before the storm. George said that most of the people here that had supported them lost their homes, too, in the storm and were relocated to other cities in the country themselves. Even though New Orleans has come a long way in repairing itself since Katrina, we still have a ways to go with some of the public services that we use to have." Charlie was silent for a moment and then said, "George did say he thought they might have something like what you're looking for in Memphis." He continued, "The only other suggestion I can think of would be a homeless shelter, but that's just food and a place to sleep."

I stood up and shook Charlie's hand. I thanked him for the help he had tried to give. As we walked back towards the front he asked, "Did you catch any fish at the lake?"

I told him of the catfish and the trout, but I wasn't as enthusiastic as I normally would be talking about fish I had caught.

As I walked back down the street towards the docks, I saw a McDonalds and stopped to pick up a couple hamburgers for dinner. As I waited on the food, I couldn't help feeling lost and confused. What the hell was I going to do? I paid for the meal and slowly walked down the street towards the Pearl. The sun was going down now and I wished the walk could have been much, much longer.

When I got back to the boat, I took a plate from the cabinet and put a hamburger and some fries on it. I squeezed a little ketchup next to the fries and sat it down in front of Yu. She was still engrossed in Mary Poppins. I poured her a glass of milk and sat it on the table. I thought to myself, she was drinking too much soda.

Yu turned around and smiled and said, "Thank you."

I looked at her bright green eyes and said, "You're more than welcome, Sweetheart." I turned back and just stared at the other hamburger. I wasn't hungry in the least. I slid it back and thought Yu could have it later. I took out a glass and filled it with ice. I poured it half full of rum then topped the rest off with soda. I pulled a chair up next to Yu and pretended to watch the movie as I sipped at my drink.

The weight of the world seemed to be sitting squarely on my shoulders. If I had not found Yu and taken her out of the swamps, she would surely be dead or dying by now. She would still be tied to that rope. I can't just kick her off the boat, or put her in some homeless shelter, but she can't stay here either. I'm single, retired and supposed to be enjoying myself alone. On top of all that, I wanted my bed back. As sweet and enjoyable as she was, she did not figure into my plans. I was definitely torn between the fact that she was young, cute, and someone you couldn't help but care for, and my old stuck-in my ways, grumpy life-style. I liked my life-style. I worked hard to get this life-style. Mary Poppins ended, so I found another movie I could pretend to watch with her. It was nine o'clock when the second movie ended. I cleared the table of dishes and put them in the sink. I escorted Yu to the bedroom and laid out the clean pair of sweatpants, socks and briefs. I said goodnight and headed for the loft again.

The next morning I awoke to the sound of the shower running. The sun was already up. I had no idea what time it was, but I was in no rush to get moving. I lay there and listened as the shower stopped and the hairdryer began. I was happy that Yu was learning how to do things for herself, and that she was getting better physically, but I also had an eerie feeling that she was becoming to attached to her new surroundings. As I lay there thinking about all that had happened, and all that may or may not happen, I heard her open the bedroom door. I could hear her small footsteps as she walked into the kitchen and opened the refrigerator. I heard the pop of a can. I laughed to myself and hoped she wasn't getting into my beer. I lay there for a moment trying to decide whether to go back to sleep or not when I heard the TV come on. Now she knows how to work the TV I thought to myself. I pulled the pillow over my head, rolled over, and went back to sleep.

When I finally did wake up, I slipped on my pants and shirt and climbed down from the loft.

Yu looked around at me and said, "Hi."

I smiled at her and said, "Good morning." I hadn't been able to take a shower yesterday and I felt it so I excused myself and walked into the bedroom closing the door behind me. I started the shower and took out clean clothes for the day. The hot water felt great, but it didn't take away the thoughts running through my mind. I had thought that I would be spending the day getting Yu settled into a new place. Now it looked as if she would be around until we could get to Memphis. That was over a thousand miles and at least ten days away. As I dried off and got dressed, I decided that I would take her shopping instead. She couldn't keep running around in those sweatpants and my underwear.

As I walked into the living room, Yu was watching a John Wayne movie. I looked down at her and said, "Would you like to go out get some breakfast and maybe do a little shopping?" Yu looked up at me, then back at the TV and then back at me again. She smiled and shook her head up and down. I took the remote and turned off the TV. I reached down and took her hand and helped her up. As we walked out onto the deck, the dockhand was standing outside his shack smoking a cigarette. Yu slid around to my left side to keep me in between her and him. I took her hand and helped her step down to the dock. As we walked up towards the street, Yu turned her head and looked back twice just to make sure he wasn't following us.

As we walked up the street, Yu continued to hold my hand. She was smiling again. Her head was like a top turning every which way looking at all the buildings and cars. I had seen a shopping mall last week when I was here and I figured they would have a dress shop some where in it. It was about six blocks from the docks, but the walk with Yu was enjoyable. She was pointing and laughing at everything. She stopped twice to look through the windows of stores as we passed. It made me feel good to see her having fun.

We were about a block away from the shopping mall when we came upon an I.H.O.P. restaurant. I almost felt devious as I lead her through the doors. Even though I had not known her for very long, I knew she was going to love this place. A young lady welcomed us as we entered and showed us to a booth. She started to hand us menus but I waved her off and said, "We will have two strawberry waffles with whipped cream and two glasses of milk. No make that chocolate milk."

The waitress smiled and said, "All-righty, I'll get that right out."

Yu was looking at everything, the ceiling, the booths and the people. The grin on her face was evidence that she liked the décor of restaurant a lot. The waitress brought our chocolate milks over and set them down. Yu looked at the brown milk with caution in her eyes. I laughed and said, "Try it" as I picked my glass up and took a sip. Yu slowly raised the glass and tried it. She started smiling and drank half of the glass before she put it down. Now she had a brown milk mustache. I laughed and handed her a napkin.

When the waitress brought our breakfasts over and set them down in front of us, I thought Yu's eyes were going to pop out of her head. I had to admit that they were huge. There were a lot of strawberries and the whipped cream was three or four inches high. I was still laughing at Yu as I reached over and poured a little syrup on her waffle. She grabbed her fork and attacked her breakfast with a vengeance. I laughed and thought to myself she sure could eat a lot for such a little girl. I was only able to eat half of my waffle before I became stuffed. Yu, on the other hand, was not about to give up. She kept plugging away without any indication that she would stop before it was all gone. I laughed as she got whipped cream on her nose and strawberries on her chin. She was making a mess, but enjoying every bite. I ordered a few more napkins.

After breakfast we continued on to the shopping mall. Yu seemed to be walking a little slower after her big breakfast. As we entered the mall, Yu was in awe of the size of the place. She let go of my hand and ran to the windows of each store we passed, looking at everything they offered inside. I found a woman's dress shop and guided Yu in. A very well dressed and nice looking lady met us as we entered. She smiled at Yu and said, "May I help you with anything in particular?"

I said, "Yes. My friend here needs some clothes." I continued, "A few pair of cotton pants with a drawstring or elastic waistband. A couple of pull over shirts or blouses, maybe one nice dress, a pair of tennis shoes, and some woman's under garments."

The lady looked at me and said, "Certainly, let's start over here." She led us over to a pants rack.

I thumbed through the pants and picked out two pair, one black and one tan. I looked at the sales woman and said, "I have no idea of her size."

She laughed and said, "We'll get that all figured out in time." We then picked out a couple of blouses and a cute dress. The sales lady said, "Lets work on these and then we'll get to the shoes later."

I said, "Ok, but she still need some under garments and I'm leaving that completely in your hands."

The woman laughed again and said, "No problem." Yu and the sales person headed off to the dressing rooms. I found a chair that faced them and settled in.

I was reading a National Geographic magazine when I looked up and saw the sales lady walk out of the dressing room. She motioned another woman over and said something to her. She then went back into the dressing room as the other woman walked away. I didn't think anything of it. I continued to read the magazine. About five minutes later I looked up and saw two police officers walking towards the dressing rooms. One was a female officer. I sat there watching and I wondered what was going on. A few minutes later the sales woman and the male officer stepped out and she pointed at me. The officer started to walk over to where I was sitting. I stood up as he approached and said, "Is there a problem, officer?" The officer asked me if I was with the young woman in the dressing room. I said, "Yes, is she ok?" He just asked me to come with him and we walked towards the dressing rooms. When we got there the sales lady, Yu, and the female officer were standing in the room.

The male officer asked me, "Can you explain this sir?" Just then the sales lady lifted the back of Yu's sweatshirt. Her back was covered with slash marks, welts and bruises. It looked as if someone had beaten her with a whip many, many times. Her back looked like a map of mountain ranges. My heart sank. I honestly wanted to cry.

I motioned for the officer to step away from the dressing rooms. As we did I told him I had nothing to do with what had happened to Yu and that I had never seen her back before. I explained what had happened in the Bayous. I told him of the reports I had given both the rangers at the lake and Detective Rogers at Precinct Three. I explained that we were there because she had no clothes of her own. He asked me to wait for a minute, as he walked away and started talking on his radio. After a few minutes he returned and said that my story had checked out. He suggested that I take Yu to a doctor and have her wounds inspected. I told him I would.

We walked back into the dressing room and he told his partner and the sales lady that everything was all right and they left. I looked at the sales lady and said, "She does need the clothes. I will get her checked out by a doctor as soon as I can."

I left the dressing room and headed back to my chair. I couldn't believe that someone could take that much abuse or that someone could be cruel enough to torture someone else that way. I knew in my heart that the search for a place to dump her was over. I would take care of Yu for the rest of my life.

Chapter 6

After we were finished getting everything we needed at the mall, Yu and I headed back towards the docks. We were on the west side of the mall when we came out so we walked down a different street on our way back to the boat. It was the usual male, female relationship. I carried all the packages and she walked along swinging her empty arms as if to say, "I have him trained well." We had only gone a couple of blocks when I discovered that God was very angry with me. Yu saw it first. It was a pet shop. Not just any old pet shop but a pet shop with a cute cocker spaniel puppy in the window. I looked up towards the sky and said, "Your timing is unbelievable."

Yu was already at the window screaming, "Look, look, puppy."

I stood there staring at the dog with Yu for a few minutes then reluctantly said, "Ok, lets go inside." I opened the door and Yu shot in like a bullet. I was thankful that there was a young lady behind the sales counter. Yu ran over to the puppy and started petting it. It was jumping up and barking as it tried to get Yu to pick it up. I walked up to the young lady behind the counter and asked, "How much is that doggie in the window?"

She laughed and said, "A hundred and twenty five dollars."

I didn't laugh. I said, "We will need a doggie bed, a couple of doggie bowls, and a bag of food also." She walked over picked up two bowls, a soft cotton bed and a bag of dog food. She put them on the counter and started ringing it all up. I put the bowls and food into the bags I was already carrying. I sat them down and handed the young lady my credit card. I then walked over to Yu and picked up the puppy and handed it to her. Yu was all smiles.

She said, "Thank you, thank you."

I said, "He's yours now. You have to take care of him."

Yu said, "Okay!"

I walked back over to the counter, signed the receipt, picked up our valuables, and grabbed the bed with the same hand as one of the bags. I thought to myself all I need now is a gun and the three promises I had made myself in the Bayous would be complete. The puppy was licking Yu all over her face as we left the store.

When we got back to the Pearl I walked in and put the bags and bed down on the kitchen table. I didn't know how it was going to work with a dog on the boat but I knew I would have to make some changes. That could come later. I had other things to take care of first. I called Yu over to the table and put my hand on her back. As I moved my hand up and down I asked her, "Does this hurt?"

Yu looked at me with trusting eyes and said, "No."

I said, "Good" and smiled at her. She smiled back and began to play with the dog again. I stepped out onto the deck and yelled over to the dockhand, "Do you have a local phone book?"

He yelled back, "Yeah."

I walked over to him and borrowed the book. I began calling female doctors on my cell phone to see if I could get Yu in today to get her back checked. I had to make a lot of calls. After finding a female doctor that could squeeze Yu in, I called a taxicab company and asked them to have a cab at the dock in an hour. I gave the dockhand back his phone book and climbed back aboard the Pearl.

I took the clothes from the table and carried them into the bedroom. I laid out a change of clothes on the bed for Yu. As I laid out the underwear and bra I was sure hoping the saleslady had shown Yu what to do with them. I called Yu into the bedroom and told her we had to go see someone and I asked her to change her clothes. I shut the bedroom door as I headed back into the living room. As I waited on Yu to get dressed I turned on the computer and pulled up my bank account. I had been spending a lot of money. I made a payment on my credit card and transferred another two thousand dollars from my savings to my checking account. I thought to myself, the way things are going, that should last me a couple more hours at least.

When Yu stepped out of the bedroom, I was amazed. The clothes fit very nicely. The baggy look was gone. She looked great. I said, "Look at you, aren't you the pretty one."

Yu smiled and said, "Pretty."

I said, "Very pretty." She turned around in a slow circle and modeled for me. Her tennis shoes were untied so I motioned for her to sit down in the kitchen chair. After she was sitting, I leaned over and very slowly tied each shoe hoping that she was watching and might be able to do it herself next time. I stood up and looked again. She was very pretty, but something was off. I looked for a moment then realized it was the hair. It was clean and dry but it hung straight down. There was no body to it. I laughed and thought, *that can be fixed later it's only money.* I set the doggie bowls on the floor with food and water and got ready to leave.

When the taxi arrived we were already on the dock waiting. As I opened the back door of the cab, Yu looked hesitant but I said, "It's ok" and she crawled in. I gave the driver the address and off we went. Yu bounced up and down on the seat looking the cab over. Then snapped her head around trying to inspect every building that we passed. I envied Yu. Everything she saw was always new and exciting. It took about ten minutes to reach the doctors office. I paid the cabby and we got out.

The waiting room was empty as we walked in. I told the receptionist who we were and we sat down to wait. A few minutes later a young woman opened the door and called, "Yu?"

I stood up and took Yu's hand and accompanied her back to the exam room. We had only been in the room a few minutes when a very lovely older black woman walked in. She extended her hand and said, "I'm Doctor Parrish."

I shook her hand and introduced Yu and myself. I asked Yu to sit there while I stepped out to talk to the doctor. We stepped out of the room and I explained to the doctor why we were there. I asked her to check Yu over everywhere, not just her back. I told her I would wait in the waiting room. The doctor smiled and said she would come get me when the exam was over. I walked back out front to wait.

Yu had been in there for about forty-five minutes. I was starting to get impatient when the door opened and the young lady said, "The doctor will see you now." I got up and walked back to the exam room. The doctor was standing outside waiting on me.

As I approached, the doctor said, "My God man, that child has been abused more than anyone I have ever seen. After you had explained what you were coming in for, I expected some scars and bruising, but nothing like what I just saw. The scars on her back are a result of multiple beatings over many years. I'm surprised she can still walk, let alone live through that kind of treatment." She continued, "The scaring seems to be confined to just her back. There was no indication of any other trauma to her legs or other extremities. I x-rayed for broken bones and found a couple of ribs that had been broken but have healed. She seems to be in good spirits and I can't find anything that would indicate she needs any immediate or long-term care." She went on, "I have some ointment here, and she handed me a large tube, that will help with the contusions on her back. It has an antibacterial formula as well as a softening agent. It will keep the skin from drying out and keep any chance of infection from starting, hopefully." She added, "You can get this over the counter just about anywhere."

I looked at the doctor and said, "Thank you so very much. Is there any chance of getting a copy of your report so I can give it to the detective that is handling her file?"

The doctor said, "Certainly" and headed off to her office.

I stepped back into the exam room. Yu looked up at me as I entered and smiled real big. I smiled back at her and said, "How do you feel?"

She answered, "Good!"

I laughed and said, "Ok, you ready to go?" She jumped down off the exam table and shook her head up and down.

We walked out to the receptionist; I paid her, and received a copy of the doctor's report. I asked the young lady if she would call us a cab and Yu and I stepped outside to wait. We hadn't been waiting very long when the cab pulled up. I helped Yu in; there was no hesitation this time. I glanced at the report and read the instructions on the tube of cream as we made the ten-minute trip back to the docks. As we got out of the cab I paid the driver and noticed a beauty shop just a couple of doors down the street. I took Yu's hand and started walking towards it. Yu looked back at the docks as we headed away from them then up to me and said, "I.H.O.P?"

I laughed and said, "Not this time. Lets go get your hair done." Yu reached up and touched her hair with her free hand and started skipping down the street beside me.

Yu and I entered the beauty shop and walked up to the counter. The lady behind the counter smiled and said, "May I help you?"

I said, "Yes ma'am, we would like to get Yu's hair cut."

The lady turned around and shouted, "Louise, are you free?" Louise waved for us to come on back. Yu and I walked back to Louise's station.

Louise patted the chair and said, "Have a seat, little lady," looking at Yu. I guided Yu into the chair, and Louise placed a smock over her, and tied it in the back. Louise said, "Mercy, girl, whose been cutting your hair, this is a mess?"

I quickly said, "It's a long story. Can you just straighten it up and give her some body and maybe a few waves?"

Louise turned the chair around to look straight at Yu's face. She studied it for a minute then glanced down at Yu's hands. She took one of Yu's hands in hers and said, "I can fix the hair, but this young lady needs a manicure real bad also."

I shook my head in disbelief and said, "Sure, why not." I asked, "How long do you think all of this will take?"

Louise studied Yu's hair again for a few seconds then turned towards me and said, "Probably a good hour, maybe a little longer."

I told Yu I would be right up front. She smiled and said, "Ok." I walked back to the front of the shop to take a seat and picked up a magazine to pass the time.

I looked up every few minutes to check on the progress. Louise had turned the chair around again and lowered it back and was washing Yu's hair. Another woman was working on her fingernails. Yu was smiling and seemed to be enjoying the pampering. Yu was in good hands and I knew the police station was only two blocks away. I could take the doctors report over to Charlie and be back long before Yu was done. I stepped up to the counter and told the lady there that I would be gone for a few minutes. If Yu asked for me, tell her I will be right back. She smiled and said she would. I slipped out the door and headed for the police station.

As I entered the precinct I walked up to the counter and asked for Detective Rogers. The officer picked up the phone, dialed and said, "Charlie, there's a guy up here that wants to see you." The officer hung up the phone and looked back at me and said, "He'll be right with you."

As Charlie came out I shook his hand and said, "I take it you heard about what happened this morning?"

Charlie had a concerned look on his face and said, "Yeah, how is she?"

I handed him the doctor's report and said, "Other than having gone through hell, she seems to be OK." I told him what the doctor had told me and asked him to include the report in his file. I said, "As bad as her back is, its possible that what happened this morning could happen again. If the report is in your file then at least who ever may be concerned about her condition will know it was not because of me."

Charlie agreed and said he would include it in the file. Then Charlie said, "I contacted the ranger station over on Lake Borgne to follow up on what was happening. They have recovered the body and it is being shipped here to New Orleans to the forensic lab. Once they find out who this guy is, maybe they can find out who the girl is." He asked, "Have you found a place that will take her yet?"

I smiled and simply said, "No, she has a home with me as long as she needs it. I can't just dump her off somewhere." I gave Charlie my cell phone number and asked him to give me a call if they did find out something about her. I shook his hand, said goodbye and headed back towards the beauty shop. When I got back to the beauty shop, the two women were still working hard on Yu; I doubt that she even knew I had left. I sat down and picked up the magazine and started reading once more.

The hour passed by slowly. I was on my fourth magazine when Yu and Louise finally approached the counter. I stood up and saw Yu walking towards me. The difference was unbelievable. It caught me by surprise. She was beautiful, not just cute. She looked as if she should be wearing designer clothes and sables. As she approached, she held her fingers out for me to see. Her fingernails were a light green that matched her sparkling green eyes. She had a huge smile on her face and said, "Pretty." I couldn't believe this was the same woman that, just five days ago, was half starved and looked like something the cat had drug in. Now you would think she had just stepped off a movie set or a runway at some fashion show. I paid the bill and tipped Louise and the lady that had done the manicure twenty dollars each. They deserved it.

Yu and I stepped out of the beauty shop and headed back towards the dock. It was after two and I knew Yu must be getting hungry by now. I was. I figured I would make us some lunch on the Pearl rather than spend any more money eating out. As we got back to the boat and opened the sliding glass doors of the cabin, Yu and I both caught our breaths in unison. There was dog food all over the floor. The puppy had crapped on the carpet and Yu's teddy bear was torn to shreds. There was stuffing everywhere. Yu stepped in and picked up what was left of the bear as the puppy barked and jumped up onto my leg in hopes of being picked up. She held it towards me almost in tears with big sad eyes. She had left it sitting on a kitchen chair. I guess the dog was able to jump up and pull it down. I took the teddy bear remains and hugged Yu. I said, "It's OK, I'll get you another one." I walked Yu out onto the front deck and sat her in a chair. The puppy followed. I asked her to keep the dog out here and I went back in to start cleaning up the mess.

After the entire cleanup had been completed, I walked back out onto the front deck where Yu had obviously forgiven the puppy for all his small indiscretions. They were playing and seemed to be having a good time. I on the other hand, knew that I had to do something about the situation. I walked back into the kitchen and made Yu and myself a sandwich. I took them and a couple of sodas back out to the table where Yu was sitting and sat down to eat while forming a plan. As we ate, an idea grew. By the time we had both finished our lunch I had it all worked out in my mind. It would be the first project I would undertake, as our new family became a reality.

I looked over at Yu and said, "You need to think of a name for the puppy."

Yu looked up at me and with a question in her eyes and asked, "Name?"

I said, "Yeah, something we can call him. Your name is Yu and my name is Terry. He needs a name and you get to decide what that name is going to be."

Yu smiled. She looked proud. Her expression said, "I get to name him!"

I said, "You think about it while I get started on some things we need to do for him around the boat." I could tell that Yu was deep in thought as I stood up and walked into the cabin. The first thing I did was to grab my tape measurer and measure the heights and lengths of all the railings on both the front and rear decks. Then I measured the width and length of the rear deck itself. I called the taxi company and requested a cab meet me at the head of the dock. I asked Yu to watch the puppy and told her that I would be gone for a while but that I would be back soon.

Yu smiled up at me as she wrestled with the dog and said, "Ok." I walked up to the head of the dock to wait on the taxi.

When the cab arrived I told the driver we had two or three different places to go. The first stop on the list was the pet shop where we had bought the dog. I picked up a doggie door and a few chew toys. Next I had the driver take me to a nursery where I bought a hundred square feet of blue grass sod, a roll of heavy black plastic, a four-foot tall tree in a round planter pot, and a small bag of bark. I paid the salesman and scheduled him to deliver the items to the dock in an hour. We then drove to a hardware store where I purchased eighty lineal feet of three foot high by one-eighth inch thick, hard clear plastic, some metal screws, and a bag of grommets. The taxi driver put the hard plastic roll in his trunk and tied the trunk lid down on top of it. We headed back to the Pearl.

I paid and tipped the driver for his patience and his help, and placed all the items I had purchased on the sidewalk next to the cab. I had to make three trips to get all the stuff down to the boat. When I had all the items onboard, I started to gather my tools together and got started. Yu and the dog were still playing on the front deck. She had a rag and was playing tug-of-war with the puppy. As I got ready to start cutting the plastic, I heard her say, "Here Blackie." She had named the dog. I started laughing hysterically. I realized that she had named him after the puppy on the Shirley Temple movie she had watched a couple of days ago. The funny part of it was that the puppy on the movie was a black lab and this one was a very light tan colored cocker spaniel. I started working, still laughing to myself.

My plan was brilliant. I was going to cover all of the railings on the front and back decks with the eighth inch hard clear plastic, so that the puppy couldn't fall overboard. Then I would put the sod and tree on the back deck so he would have a real back yard to play and relieve himself on. The doggie door would go in the back door leading out of the bedroom to the grassy playground. I was almost finished with the plastic on the back deck when I saw the nursery truck pull up at the head of the docks.

I left the Pearl and walked up to sign for the delivery. The delivery driver wheeled the sod and the tree down to the Pearl using a hand truck and stacked it on the dock next to the rear deck. I brought the small bag of bark and the roll of plastic with me as I followed him down. I tipped the driver and thanked him for his help. I returned to the front deck and asked Yu to come with me. I took her into the bedroom and asked her to change back into the sweatpants outfit. She looked at me as if I were crazy but started to do so as I closed the door and waited in the kitchen. When she had changed I took her out on the back deck.

I stepped off onto the dock and picked up a square of sod and handed it up to her through the railing gate. Her sweatshirt was instantly covered in dirt from the sod. I motioned for her to set it down on the deck and continued to hand her sod until all the sod was onboard. I lifted the tree up and set it on the deck. I jumped back aboard and slid the tree to the back of the deck. I walked over to Yu laughing and brushed some of the dirt off her shirt. I looked at her and said, "You can change your clothes again now." She didn't laugh or smile. She just walked back into the cabin, the puppy at her feet, and closed the door behind her. I was still laughing out loud as I continued my work.

I finished the hard plastic on the railings and walked over to the tree. I measured the diameter of the pot and cut a hole in the deck that cantilevered out past the engine. The hole I cut was about two feet back from both the rear and right-hand side railings. I could see the water below; through the hole I had just cut. I slid the round container that the tree was in, over and slowly lowered it into the hole. The molded ring at the top of the container sat firmly on the deck, not allowing the tree to fall through.

I then began to lay the heavy black plastic, covering the entire area. I over-lapped it so that any water would run off the back or sides of the deck and not be able to soak into the carpeting or the wood below. Then I started laying the sod. It went down very quickly and easily. When I reached the tree I covered the ring of the container with the sod but cut a circle around the inside of the pot exposing the soil the tree was in. I filled the void between the soil and the top of the sod with the bark. As I finished I stood up, stepped back and looked at my work. It was great. It turned out better than I had imagined it would. It was a real back yard.

It was almost five thirty when I finished putting in the doggie door. The sun would be down in just a little while. I was tired and covered with dirt but I felt proud of the work I had done. I cleaned up the extra pieces of sod and plastic and put my tools away. I dusted myself off as best I could. I was excited and in a hurry to show Yu what I had accomplished before it got dark. I felt like a school kid wanting to impress some cute little girl on the playground. I walked through the cabin to the front deck where Yu and the puppy were still at war with the rag. Yu was still wearing the sweatpants and sweatshirt. I motioned for her to follow me back out to the rear deck. As we walked through the bedroom I opened the back door and we stepped out into our new back yard. Yu looked amazed and walked over to the tree to touch it. She then kneeled down and rubbed her hand over the grass. She looked up at me and smiled with approval. Blackie was running around sniffing everything. Then suddenly he stopped, squatted and began to pee. I started laughing. It was a success already.

    I told Yu I would be right back. I walked into the kitchen, filled Blackie's bowls up with food and water, and then carried them back out to where Yu and he were playing with the new chew toys I had bought. I put the bowls down on the grass against the back wall of the bedroom. Blackie ran over and started drinking. I looked around and started thinking to myself that we needed another picnic table and chairs with an umbrella out here, since the back deck, I mean backyard was uncovered. I had a feeling we would be using the backyard a lot more now.

    I reached down and picked Blackie up as he was still drinking from his bowl. I walked over to the back door and pushed him through the doggie door into the bedroom. Yu didn't seem to understand what I had done or why I had done it. I waited a second then lifted the rubber doggie door up and called Blackie back outside. He came running back through. Yu smiled. I kept pushing Blackie through the doggie door and calling him until he finally pushed the door open himself and came through without any assistance from me. Now we were getting somewhere. The sun was starting to set, so Yu and I went into the cabin, leaving Blackie out in the backyard. Yu seemed distressed at that fact, but I called for Blackie and, even though it took a few seconds, he finally stuck his head through the doggie door and came running through to join us. Yu grabbed him up in her arms and the two of them started trading kisses. I started dinner.

We ate our dinner on the front deck. I had a Tony Bennett CD playing softly on the CD player. As the lights of the city shined across the water of the Mississippi, and with Blackie sound asleep at Yu's feet, we listened to the music gently drift across the river. It was turning into a perfect evening. As I sat there listening to the music and thinking of days gone by, I stood up and took Yu's hand. I gently pulled her up from her seat and put my left arm around her tiny waist and placed her right hand in mine. As I stared into her beautiful green eyes I gently moved her around the deck, dancing to the rhythm of the master. I felt like I was Fred Astaire and she was Ginger Rogers, floating gently across the stage in some old and famous movie. It was the perfect end to a very long day.

A few hours later we called it an evening and headed to bed. I put the dog's bed on the floor in the bedroom with Yu. Since she was still wearing the sweatpants outfit, I thought that this would be a good time to put the medication on her back. I had her lay down on the bed with her back facing up. I squeezed the medicine out of the tube into my hand and gently lifted her sweatshirt and started rubbing the cream all over her mutilated back. I could feel every hit of the whip as I spread the salve over her scars. Yu lay there with her eyes closed and seemed to like the feeling of the moist cream soaking into her skin. When I felt that I had covered all of her wounds, I lowered her shirt, and stepped into the bathroom to wash my hands.

As I returned to the bedroom, Yu was already under the covers smiling and ready for bed. She was still wearing the sweatpants and sweatshirt that she helped me unload the sod with. I knew I would have to wash the bedclothes tomorrow. I thought to myself that I needed to take her shopping again and get her a pair of pajamas. I said goodnight, closed the door, and climbed up to the loft. As I lay there thinking of the events of the day I could hear Blackie barking in the bedroom. I knew that I would have to listen to it all night long. Suddenly the barking stopped. I thought for a second then started laughing to myself realizing that Yu had picked the dog up and put it in bed with her. I smiled, rolled over, drifted off to sleep, and dreamed of green eyes.

The next morning I was up before Yu and Blackie. I started cooking some ham and eggs. I had originally planed on leaving today. I had planed on leaving by myself, but obviously those plans had changed. So I decided we would stay one more night and leave in the morning. That would give me a chance to catch up on a few things I still needed to finish, like laundry and the plastic on the front deck. I had just started the hash browns when I heard the shower start. If I timed this just right, breakfast would be ready just as Yu walked out of the bedroom. I sat the table and filled a couple glasses of milk. Time flew by as I flipped the hash browns and scrambled the eggs. I had just taken Yu's plate off the table and was filling it with the food when the bedroom door opened and Yu stepped out. Damn I'm good, I thought to myself. Yu was wearing the dress we had bought yesterday. *She obviously has no plans to help me finish the plastic around the front deck*, I mused. I sat her plate on the table and held her chair out for her. When she was seated I grabbed Blackie, who was at her feet, and put him out back and locked the doggie door. I served up my breakfast and joined Yu at the table.

When breakfast was over, Yu started cleaning up and washing the dishes while I started working on the plastic on the front deck. It took a couple hours to finish, but now Blackie was totally safe from falling over board. I cleaned up my mess and jumped into the shower.

After I was dressed, we locked Blackie back out in the back yard, caught a cab, and Yu and I went shopping. We went back to the nursery and picked out a nice round picnic table and padded chairs for the back yard. It had an umbrella. I scheduled it to be delivered later that day. We then had the cabbie take us back to the mall. We thanked him and paid him, we could walk home from here. We spent the next few hours walking the mall looking in all the shops. We found her another teddy bear that looked just like the first one, only bigger. We went back to the women's store that we had bought the clothes from the day before to pick up a pair of pajamas. As we entered a pretty young girl walked up to us and asked, "May I help you find something?"

As I started to answer her, the sales lady that helped us yesterday stepped up and said, "I'll help these people, Janet, their friends of mine." Then she looked at Yu and said, "My, don't you look nice today. And I love what you have done with your hair."

Yu smiled, touched her hair and said, "Pretty!"

I figured we would only be in the shop for a few minutes to get a pair of pajamas. I was wrong. An hour later we walked out with two pair of pajamas, a white fluffy bath robe, a pair of house slippers with puppy's heads on them that barked when you walked, another two pair of pants, and two more blouses, not to mention a large supply of women's under garments. I would have to transfer some more money, from my savings account again when we got back to the Pearl.

As we were about to leave the mall and head for home we passed a cotton candy cart. Yu watched in amazement as the young woman spun the sugary glass candy around the paper cone. I laughed at Yu all the way back to the Pearl. By the time we had walked two blocks she had the cotton candy all over herself. She was picking it out of her beautiful new hairstyle and her pretty green fingertips were turning a sugary red. She was definitely going to need a shower when we got back.

The Rope

We hadn't been back on the boat for long when the picnic table, chairs and umbrella arrived. The driver helped me carry them down to the boat and place them in the back yard. It was perfect. Yu smiled and sat in each of the four chairs. I opened the umbrella above the table and it shaded the table and chairs exactly as I had hoped it would. I went into the kitchen and got us a couple of drinks and took them back out to the new playground. Yu and I sat there for about an hour, just enjoying our new furniture, as Blackie played on the grass with his chew toys.

Later that afternoon as Yu took a shower to try to get the cotton candy out of her hair, I gathered up all the dirty clothes, bed sheets and pillowcases, and took them to a Laundromat. I left Yu and Blackie behind to hold down the fort on the Pearl while I was gone. As I waited on the clothes, I went across the street to a small tackle shop and did some shopping for myself. I picked up another nice little rod and reel and some needed tackle. When all was done the four-block walk back to the Pearl was somewhat of a hassle. Trying to carry all the fishing equipment and clothes at the same time was uncomfortable, and awkward, to say the least. I finally made it without dropping a thing. We spent the rest of the afternoon and evening sitting in the back yard playing with Blackie and later watching TV in the living room. It had turned out to be another very nice day.

The next morning, we topped off with fuel and water, paid our mooring charges, and headed north, up the Mississippi River. We spent the next three weeks fishing, swimming, relaxing and just plain having fun. We even spent three days exploring Profit Island where Blackie chased everything that crawled, flew or had four legs. We stopped a number of times along the way for supplies, to do laundry, and just to see the sights. This had been my original plan. But I have to admit it was much more enjoyable doing it with Yu and Blackie.

One afternoon we came into Natchez, Mississippi. It was only about three o'clock but the sky was filled with dark, threatening looking clouds. We decided it would be wise to tie up here for the night. Blackie was running short on dog food so Yu and I decided to walk into town, look around a bit, and pick him up some on our way back. We had walked about a mile away from the Pearl when I saw a country western bar that advertised live music. I thought Yu might like to see real people actually singing and playing the instruments that she had been listening to on the CD player. So I took her hand and we walked towards the bar.

As we entered the bar I was surprised to see that it was much larger than it had appeared from the outside. The decor was that of an old Honky-Tonk that you might see in an old western movie. The bartender and waitresses were dressed in outfits of that era. There were portraits of old time dancing girls and pictures of the streets of Natchez, back when the road out front of the bar was still dirt, hanging on the walls. There were bullet holes in the ceiling and walls and I wasn't quite sure if they were real or just décor. There were a lot of people there. I couldn't see one empty table. The band that was playing on stage sounded great. It looked like everyone was having a good time.

I found Yu and I a couple of stools at the end of the bar and helped her up on hers. I ordered a light beer for myself and a Shirley Temple for her. We sat there listening to the music for over an hour. Yu was clapping to the beat and swaying to the music. I was on my third beer and Yu was on her second Shirley Temple. She seemed to be enjoying herself immensely and I was in no hurry to get back to the Pearl either. The band announced that they were going to take a fifteen-minute pause for the cause. I thought that was a great idea after the three beers, so I told Yu that I would be back in a minute and headed for the restroom.

I was only gone for a few minutes. As I came back out of the small hallway the restrooms were located in, I saw Yu flying off her bar stool, hitting the floor and wall as she covered or held the left side of her face. There was a large man with a ponytail, leather vest, blue jeans, and biker boots standing over her. I was at the bar in a second. I grabbed the man by his right shoulder, spun him around, and hit him as hard as I could. I caught him square on the jaw. He fell back and hit the floor with a loud thud. The bar became silent. Every head in the place was staring at us, to see what was going on. The man was much younger and a lot bigger than I was, but I knew in my heart he would not be walking out of here on his own two feet tonight. I was ready for the fight. As I started towards him to finish the job, he held his arm out towards me and started yelling, "Man, I didn't do anything."

Another man that was sitting at the bar jumped up in front of me, holding me back, and said, "He's telling the truth. All he did was touch your friend on the shoulder and asked her if that bar stool was empty. She freaked out."

I stood there for a second waiting for the biker to make any type of a move. My heart was still pumping ninety miles an hour. My fist was cocked and my adrenalin was still screaming fight. I backed up, looked at the man that had jumped up from the bar, then back at the biker. I lowered my fist, turned and went to Yu. I picked her up off the floor. She was shaking like a leaf. I threw a fifty dollar bill on the bar and told the bar tender to buy the biker his drinks as I walked Yu to the front door past him. He still laying on the floor rubbing his chin. I didn't look at him or apologize as we left.

As we started the long walk back to the Pearl, it started to sprinkle. Yu was walking very close to me holding my arm very tight with both hands. We were three blocks away from the bar and she was still shaking. It was my fault. I should never have put her in that situation. She had seemed to be doing much better but obviously she was still having issues. I was cursing myself. If I could, I would have taken myself out behind the bar and kicked the living crap out of me. I honestly deserved nothing less. When we finally reached the Pearl we were both soaked to the bone. I left Yu standing in the living room as I went to the back door and opened it. Blackie was lying under the table trying to stay dry. Upon seeing the door open and me standing there, he bolted into the cabin. I walked back to Yu and with my arms around her we walked into the bedroom. I handed her a towel, told her to get out of her wet clothes, and change into something dry. I walked back into the kitchen with a towel, closing the door behind me. I opened the fridge and popped the top on a can of soda.

The bedroom door opened and Yu walked out in her pajamas and doggie slippers. The shoes barked as she walked over to me, put her head on my chest, wrapped both arms around me, and held me very tightly. With one hand holding her back, I stroked her still wet hair with the other. We stood there holding each other in silence for a long time. She felt so fragile and she was. I couldn't help but think to myself, she should be angry. She should be hitting me, not holding me. I was responsible for her pain. I had been careless. I should have protected her; instead I fed her to the wolves. I had let her down. I made a promise to her, and to myself silently, as we stood there holding each other that I would never let her down like that again. As God as my witness, I would never let that happen again.

It was only a little after six but when Yu finally let me go, she walked into the bedroom, pulled off her shoes, and crawled into bed. I followed her and covered her with the blankets. The rain was coming down hard now so I stepped out into the back yard and brought Blackie's bowls in. I carried them to the sink and poured the water out and dumped the soggy dog food into the trash. I refilled them both and sat them on the kitchen floor. I sneaked back into the bedroom and grabbed some dry clothes. As I closed the bedroom door behind me, I quietly walked into the living room to change. Blackie was eating his food but stopped long enough to look up at me like he knew I had screwed up. I changed my clothes, turned on the news, and sat there drinking my soda as Blackie chewed on his toy at my feet.

Chapter 7

The next morning I awoke as the sun came in through the window. The rain had stopped. I climbed down from the loft and was surprised to see Blackie asleep under the kitchen table. The dog was smarter than I was. He had let Yu sleep. He put her needs above his own wants. I got dressed and walked into town. I found a super market and picked up the dog food we had originally gone out for the night before. While I was there, I picked up some pastries and a vase full of flowers. When I got back to the Pearl it was still quiet. Yu was still asleep. I placed the flowers on the kitchen table and the pastries on the counter. I slipped the dog food into the cabinet then walked outside and untied the Pearl. I came back in and started the engine. I headed up the river. I wanted to get as far away from Natchez as I could before Yu woke up. I honestly didn't know if our leaving there was for her sake or for mine.

We had been gone for about a half hour. Yu was still asleep. It bothered me that she was sleeping this long, knowing she had gone to bed so early, but I didn't want to wake her. Blackie was awake but still lying quietly under the kitchen table. I figured if he had an accident, I would just have to clean it up. I didn't want to open the bedroom door to let him out back and take the chance of waking Yu. He seemed to understand. Even the Pearl hummed along quietly as if she knew that Yu was not to be disturbed. We continued slowly heading north against the current.

The sun was starting to appear over the tops of the trees on the east side of the river. It looked like the storm had passed and it was going to be a pretty day. I was still thinking about Yu and last night when I heard my cell phone start ringing. I frantically started searching for it, following the sound. I finally found it under a rag on the counter top and pushing the button I said, "Hello!"

The voice on the phone said, "Terry, this is Detective Rogers in New Orleans."

I replied, "Charlie! How are you? I didn't know cops got up this early!"

Charlie laughed and said, "Yeah, there are some of us poor stiffs out here that still have to work for a living." He continued, "Listen, the reason I'm calling is that forensics finally finished its DNA on the body from the shack. It turns out that his name was Jean Paul Lafayette. This guy had a rap sheet four inches thick. It goes all the way back to when he was eleven years old. He has been arrested at one time or another for everything you can think of. Burglary, armed robbery, kidnapping, assault, rape and he was serving a life sentence in Angola for the murder of a woman and her six year old child when he escaped back in nineteen eighty-eight. They never caught him or found a body so after a few years of not hearing anything about him, they wrote him off as possibly having died in the escape attempt. This was one bad dude. He once beat a man with a tire iron, breaking both his arms and legs, just because he walked in front of his truck as he was about to pull out of a parking lot." Charlie went on, "He was sixty-four when he died. He has one living relative -- a younger sister, fifty-eight, that lives in Mobil, Alabama. We contacted her and she had not heard from him or seen him in over thirty-five years. When we asked her what she wanted done with the body she just said,

"Burn the son-of-a-bitch. I don't want to have anything thing to do with him." and hung up on us."

I listened in amazement. Charlie went on, "We couldn't find anything that said he had a daughter or a wife so I still can't tell you anything about who the girl you found with him might be. Maybe she was a girlfriend."

I interrupted Charlie and said, "I doubt that very seriously."

Charlie asked, "Is she still with you?"

I said, "Yes."

He said, "Well, I just wanted to touch base with you and let you know what we had found out so far. If I get any new information that might help you, I'll call you back."

I thanked Charlie for what he was doing for Yu and I and told him to give my best to Frank. I hung up and wondered what life must have been like for Yu while she was with this Jean Paul Lafayette? It must have been hell.

It was almost nine o'clock when Blackie and I heard the movement in the bedroom. Blackie jumped up from where he was lying under the kitchen table and walked out to sit in the living room hallway staring intently at the bedroom door. As we heard the shower start, Blackie looked up at me as if asking, "How long is this going to take?"

The river had widened to a point where it looked more like a lake than it did the river. I saw a small beach on the west side of the river that was tucked back in a large lagoon that looked like it would be a good spot to stop for a while. I headed the Pearl in that direction. As we neared the beach I throttled back on the engine and softly slid the pontoons of the Pearl up on the sandy shoreline. I shut the engine off, went to the front deck, and grabbed the mooring line. I jumped onto the bank and I tied the line to a near-by tree. Then I pulled the walk plank out from beneath the front deck and stretched it onto the sandy beach. Blackie shot by me like a rocket and headed for the near-by tree line. As I walked back into the cabin, the shower had stopped and

I could hear the sound of the hairdryer coming from the bathroom. It was about five minutes after the hairdryer stopped that Yu finally stepped out of the bedroom door. She looked radiant. I said, "Good morning Sunshine."

She smiled and softly said, "Hi!" She walked over to where I was standing and put her arms around me, laid her head on my chest, and hugged me like she had done the night before. I wrapped both my arms around her and hugged her back. If nothing else, I was very confused at her behavior. But I liked the feel of her in my arms and I wasn't about to do or say anything to stop it. I just stood there holding her and wished somehow it wouldn't end.

When it did, she took a step backwards. I looked down at her glowing face and those captivating green eyes and asked, "Are you hungry?" She was still smiling at me as she silently shook her head from side to side. Just then she saw the flowers on the kitchen table.

Her eyes got big, her mouth opened wide, and she said, "Oh! Pretty!" She let go and slid around me, walked to the table to touch and smell the flowers. I laughed and thought to myself, "Man, I am getting good." I took a plate from the cabinet and put one of the pastries I had bought on it. I grabbed a couple of sodas from the fridge and told Yu to bring the vase of flowers as I lead her out to the back yard. The sun was well up over the trees now and the morning light glimmered off the lagoon like yellow diamonds dancing on the water. There was a smell of honeysuckle in the air. I sat the plate and soft drinks on the picnic table and opened the umbrella. I held Yu's chair as she sat down and she placed the vase of flowers on the table near the umbrella pole. I put the plate with the cream puff and a soda in front of her. I opened her drink then sat down across from her as I opened mine. Blackie ran out from the cabin through the doggie door, looking very relieved after his trip to the beach and jumped into Yu's lap. As she smiled, petted and kissed Blackie, I could tell she had put last night behind her. She seemed happy and that's all that mattered to me. My worries slowly started to disappear as I watched her and Blackie love on each other.

As Yu and Blackie played, I got up and walked out to the front deck. I picked out the new light rod and reel that I had bought back in New Orleans and set it up with a single hook. I placed a split shot about six inches up from the hook and a bobber about two feet up. As I walked back towards to the backyard, I took out some cheese from the refrigerator. As I returned to the picnic table, I told Yu that I was going to teach her how to fish. I put some cheese on the hook and cast it out about fifteen feet from the Pearl. I handed her the pole and told her to watch the bobber. I sat back down and took a sip of my soft drink.

The sun was well up over us now and the shade from the umbrella felt good. The line had not been in the water long when Yu started yelling and pointing at the bobber. It was dancing across the lagoon bobbing up and down. I pointed to the reel and told her to turn the handle to bring in the line. She started turning the handle of the reel and when she felt the fish fighting on the end of the line, she started screaming and laughing. I could see it was a small fish, but the way she jumped up and fought it, you would have thought it was a marlin. When she got the fish up to the boat, she raised the tip of the pole and swung the fish around and let it drop onto the grass. Blackie ran over to the flopping fish and started sniffing at it. I chased him away and picked it up. It was a nice little brim. Yu was ecstatic.

I went back out to the front deck and got a cutting board and a knife from the cleaning table. I took it back out to the back yard and set it on the picnic table and cut the brim up into small pieces for bait. I re-baited Yu's hook and cast the line out for her again. It only took a minute then the fight was on once more. Yu screamed and laughed as she reeled the second fish in. It was about a two-pound catfish. As I took the fish off the hook I said,

"We can do better than this," and I dropped it back into the water. I re-bated the hook and cast the line back out once more. After a couple more fish I showed Yu how to cast the line out herself, and after a few attempts, she had it down pat. She didn't need my help at all after that. Yu caught fish after fish. We cut up the small ones for bait and let the rest go. I sat there drinking my soda while she fished and laughed for the next two hours. It was turning out to be a very enjoyable morning.

We spent the rest of the day walking and exploring the beach. We walked hand in hand and laughed at Blackie as he chased a squirrel, then an armadillo. Yu busted out laughing when we saw a cottonmouth swim out into the water and I jumped to her other side for protection. Snakes didn't seem to bother her at all and she laughed, turned and pointed at me, and started yelling, "Terry afraid, Terry afraid."

I was laughing too, as I answered her, "I just slipped; really I just slipped."

We walked for miles along the shoreline, holding hands and enjoying each other's company. As we walked, the sandy beach had changed and turned back into a hard grassy riverbank. We hadn't walked far on a small path that ran along the bank when the grassy shoreline rose up about three feet from the water. The muddy bank dropped straight down and laughingly I looked at Yu and said, "Watch this." I pulled off my shoes and socks and Tee shirt and waded into the muddy water of the Mississippi river. The water there was waist deep and I slowly started running my hands along the muddy bank wall under the water until I found a hole. Yu could not see what my hands were doing under the water as I reached into the hole and felt the head of a fairly large catfish. I poked at its mouth until he opened it, then I shoved my right hand into its mouth and grabbed the fish by its gills just as I had with the one back in the Bayous. The fight was on. I struggled to pull the catfish out of his hole. Yu had no idea what I was doing and looked frightened that I might be in trouble. I finally was able to dislodge the big fish, pulled it out, and lifted it up out of the water. It was about ten pounds, much smaller than the one that had almost broken my arm, and Yu was amazed at my accomplishment. She started laughing and clapping as I slipped my hand out of the catfish's mouth and let it go. I was soaked to the bone as I climbed back up to the path to rejoin Yu. The sun was warm and I knew it would not take long to dry off. I looked at her with a big smile on my face and proudly informed her, "That's what you call, noodeling." Yu was still laughing and impressed as I picked up my shoes, socks and Tee shirt and carried them with us as we headed back down the path towards the Pearl.

As the day faded into evening, I was wishing from my heart that I could hold the sun back some how for just a little while longer. It had been a wonderful day and I didn't want it to end. As we arrived back at the beach the Pearl was anchored at, the sun was setting but it was still light out. I had dried off enough to slip my socks, shoes and Tee shirt back on. I dug a small pit in the sand close to the boat and surrounded it with rocks that I gathered from the dirt beyond the tree line. I raced to gather enough fire wood before it got too dark. I started a fire then went back aboard the Pearl and got a blanket, an ice chest full of hot dogs, buns, marshmallows and soda pops, and took a couple of wire coat hangers out of the closet. I carefully carried the items back out onto the beach, where Yu and Blackie were waiting. I spread the blanket out for Yu and I to sit on. I straightened the coat hangers out and put a hot dog on the end of each one. I took Yu's hand and holding the coat hanger with the hot dog; I showed her how to hold it over the fire so it would cook. I opened a soda and placed it down in the sand next to her. We sat there laughing as Yu turned the coat hanger over a number of times, making sure that she had cooked both sides of the Oscar Meyer™ wiener well enough. I tossed Blackie a raw hot dog as we cooked our dinner and laughed as the sun faded out of sight behind us.

The fire in the pit lit up the beach around us like sparkling diamonds scattered on the ground. The darkness of night slowly replaced the light of day. Blackie had tired of chasing birds and lizards and was curled up asleep next to the blanket near Yu. Yu and I had eaten a couple of hot dogs each and now she was roasting the marshmallows that were in the ice chest. She would bust out laughing each time she held the marshmallow a little too close to the fire and it would burst into flames. She would quickly pull the burning mass of sugar towards herself and blow it out. As she popped the marshmallow into her mouth, the gooey substance muffled her laughter. She was on her way to cremating her sixth marshmallow. She brought it back towards us to take it off the coat hanger when the slippery mass of confection dropped off and landed on the blanket between us. We both reached for it at the same time. We found our faces just inches from each other staring into one another's eyes. The laughter slowly stopped and the smiles began to fade from our faces. I stared deep into her beautiful green eyes and I couldn't help myself. I slowly leaned forward and gently pressed my lips to hers. In tandem we put our arms around each other and she pulled me close as she returned my gentle embrace.

The stars were shining brightly above the blanket we laid on. We held each other tightly in a passion that had been growing for both of us, it seemed, for over a month now. My heart beat wildly, like a drum against my chest. The feelings I had been nurturing for Yu, poured out like wine from an open carafe. As we paused to catch our breaths, I looked deep into her eyes. I slowly stood up gently pulling her up with me. I placed my arm around her shoulder, pulling her close to me, and with both her arms around my waist; we slowly walked back onto the Pearl. As we entered the bedroom I closed the door behind us, leaving

Blackie to fend for himself. I never thought it would feel so good to be back in my own bed again, but it surely did tonight.

We kept the Pearl tied to that same beach for the next two weeks. Time seemed to stand still. We took long walks every day, holding on to each other as if tomorrow didn't matter. Yu caught lots of fish with her newly acquired spinning outfit. She became as good, if not better, with the rod and reel as me. Blackie explored ever inch of the shoreline and grew at an alarming rate. We cooked out on the sandy beach every night beneath the stars and the blanket became our favorite spot of all. The time we spent together there was what fairy tails are written about. I was a king and she was my queen. I had been married a long time ago and I thought I knew what love was all about. But I found out here in this small sleepy lagoon that I really was in love for the first time in my life. I started praying again each night and thanked God for letting me get lost in the Bayous. Yu truly was a miracle.

When we did finally leave the lagoon, we spent the next four weeks slowly cruising up the Mississippi river. We stopped and fished, camped out on the banks, walked through the little towns we came to, taking our time, and not wanting to miss anything. I even taught Yu how to ride a bicycle when we found a bike rental shop in one of the small towns we stopped at. We rented kayaks and paddled all over a lake we found that had a wonderful little marina. Blackie was always included. Everything we did, we did together. It was just the three of us. Each night before we went to bed, I would rub the cream onto Yu's back. I could tell it was working because her skin was getting softer and the scars seemed to be getting smaller. Life was sweet; it couldn't have been any better. But that was all about to change.

Chapter 8

Yu and I were moored at a small marina on the east side of Mud Island, just on the outskirts of Memphis, Tennessee. It had been two and a half months and a thousand miles since New Orleans. The weather was warming up nicely. Spring was here and I was trying to catch dinner as I sat on the front deck of the Pearl with Blackie. Blackie was attacking one of his chew toys as he lay at my feet. Yu was in the cabin, cleaning up the dishes from lunch, and watching the news on CNN. I could feel something playing with my bait on the line of the pole that my father had given me. I sat forward in my chair and got ready to set the hook when he took it. Just then I heard the dishes breaking on the kitchen floor and Yu let out a scream. I dropped the pole and ran into the cabin. I was afraid that Yu had cut or hurt herself somehow. She was crouched on her knees crying hysterically next to the sink where she had been working. There were broken pieces of glass and dishes all around her. I kneeled and took her shoulders in my hands and asked, "What happened, Sweetheart? Are you hurt?"

Yu just pointed at the TV and still crying hysterically said, "Popsicle."

I helped her to her feet and held her tightly. She was crying even harder now and kept repeating Popsicle. I had no idea what she was talking about, but she was starting to go limp in my arms. I swung my arm underneath her legs and picked her up. I carried her to the bedroom and laid her on the bed. She was crying uncontrollably. I sat beside her trying to calm her down, but nothing seemed to work. The more I questioned her the harder she cried. I checked her over for cuts or wounds but found none. What ever had upset her came from the TV. I covered her up with the bedspread as she lay there crying herself out. I sat there on the edge of the bed, trying my best to comfort her. She cried for a long time. She was still whimpering, but I could tell the exhaustion was taking an effect. Her body was shutting down and she was falling asleep. I sat there wondering to myself what was going on.

When I felt she was asleep and OK, I walked back into the kitchen leaving the bedroom door open. I had to find out what had caused her to react this way. I picked up the TVs remote. I had a digital recorder hooked up to the satellite receiver. I knew that it would have recorded back thirty minutes of whatever Yu had been watching. I hit record and backed the program up as far as it would go. This took it back to before I had walked outside to fish. I watched it intently, always listening for sounds that might come from the bedroom. I watched it all the way up to where I had come in after she had started screaming. I didn't see a thing that could explain her getting that upset. I even watched the commercials closely and there were no mentions of Popsicles or even ice cream. I watched it over and over. There was a small plane that made an emergency landing on a highway in Alabama, but the pilot and female passenger walked away unhurt. There was another Governor announcing his run for the two thousand eight Presidential elections and they announced the Lotto winner from last night. That was it. I was bewildered. I cleaned up the broken dishes and glass on the kitchen floor then took a chair and sat it in the hallway outside the bedroom pointing towards the bed. I kept a close eye on Yu as she slept.

The afternoon slowly turned into evening and the evening into night. I sat there watching and listening for any movement or sound from the bed. Yu never moved or uttered a word. I couldn't for the life of me figure out what could have caused her to completely fall apart this way. I had been sitting there for almost eight hours now and I was getting tired myself. I stood up and started turning out lights. As I shut the sliding glass doors and locked it, I looked out on the front deck and noticed that the fishing pole I had been using was gone. It was the one my father had given me, but it was not important right now. After everything was locked up and turned off I returned to my chair. I pulled a small comforter off the bed and draped it over my chest and legs. Blackie lay at my feet knowing something was wrong. I leaned my head against the closet door and drifted off to sleep.

It was still dark when Yu's voice woke me up. As I tried to shake the cobwebs from my head, I realized that she was kneeling in front of the chair I was sitting in with her hands holding mine on my lap. Her eyes were still filled with tears as she softly said, "Terry, it was my father and mother on the television." Not really comprehending the implications of what she had just told me, the first thing that caught my attention was the fact that she had spoken a complete sentence.

I looked at her and as I held her hands in mine, still fighting to wake up, I asked, "Are you all right Sweetheart?"

She didn't answer and she started softly crying again. She pulled a hand away and tried to wipe her runny nose. I reached into my back pocket, pulled out my handkerchief, and gently held it up to her face. She took it from my hand and blew her nose as politely as she could. She laid her head again in my lap as she started crying softly once more. I sat there with her head in my lap, softly stroking her hair with one hand, and holding her other hand in mine. We stayed like that for a long time and then she slowly raised her head and looked at me. With tears still rolling down her cheeks she very quietly and in a chocking voice said, "My name is Catherine." She put her head back down on my lap and began to cry again. I didn't know what to say or even what to think about what she had just said. My only concern was for her. I looked at my watch. It was two-thirty in the morning. I slowly stood up, raising her to her feet, and again picked her up and placed her on the bed. I laid down next to her and held her as she cried herself back to sleep. Some time after she had drifted off, I also fell back to sleep.

The sound of Blackie going out the doggy door awakened me. It was already light out. I slowly pulled my arm from beneath Catherine's pillow and looked at my watch. It was seven a.m. I slowly, quietly rolled off the bed. I was still dressed and even wearing my shoes. I walked into the kitchen and opened the refrigerator and took out a Pepsi®. The carbonation and chill of the soda felt good in my mouth and the caffeine helped me to wake up. I still didn't understand all that had happened last night, or what Catherine had said, but it was very clear that she was starting to remember things. Like what her real name was. All at once I knew I would miss the name Yu. It was just then that the fear started to run through me. I realized that she might have a life out there that didn't include me. The thought of her leaving panicked me. My knees became wobbly and I started shaking. I rushed to the sink and started splashing water on my face. I had to get a hold of myself. I told myself that I didn't know anything yet and to start thinking the worst was foolish. This could be a good thing, especially for Yu. Or should I say Catherine? I started to calm down. I had to keep my thoughts clear if I was going to help her with all she was going through. I pushed the fear of her leaving me to the back of my mind. But I knew in my heart that it was still there.

It was a few minutes later that I heard Catherine call my name. I walked quickly into the bedroom and sat on the edge of the bed. Catherine's eyes were still bloodshot, but she wasn't crying anymore. I looked at her and said, "Good morning, Sweetie."

She looked up at me and smiled as she answered, "Good morning." Her smile faded and her eyes began to water again as she asked, "Are you mad at me?"

Tears almost came to my eyes as I replied, "What would ever give you that idea?" I continued, "I could never be mad at you. I have only known happiness since the day I met you."

Her smile returned as she sat up and held me very tightly. Then she quietly said, "I love you." My heart almost jumped out of my chest. She had never said that before. I held onto her like I would never let her go.

We held and kissed each other for a very long time. Finally I pulled back a little and looked at her. We both had tears in our eyes as we started to smile, then laugh, together. I asked her if she was hungry.

She flashed that big smile and answered, "I'm so hungry I could eat a horse." The sudden change in her dialog was amazing, but I liked it a lot. I told her to shower and get changed and I would start breakfast. I kissed her again then walked back into the kitchen closing the bedroom door behind me. As I pulled out skillets and frying pans I heard the shower start. The fears, still in the back of my head, got a lot smaller. I was humming as I started the sausage and eggs, fried potatoes, toast and whipped up the pancake batter. I was cooking a feast.

Breakfast was only half done when the shower stopped and the hairdryer started. A few minutes latter Catherine opened the door and stepped out with Blackie beside her. I let go of what I was doing, turned and took her in my arms and kissed her. I looked at those beautiful green eyes and said, "You sure are pretty."

Catherine smiled and replied, "You're biased." Then she walked over and sat down at the table. I thought to myself, this actually having a conversation was going to take some getting use to. But I think I like it.

I returned to the stove, looked at her, and asked, "Would you like a soda or milk?"

Catherine replied, "Milk, please."

I couldn't help laughing to myself and thinking, what a difference a day makes. As I stirred the eggs I looked over and asked, "Did anyone ever call you Cathy, or Kate?"

Catherine got a stern look on her face and said, "Only if they were tired of living!"

I made a mental note, "No Cathy or Kate."

After breakfast was over, there was a ton of food left. I had made way to much. But I didn't care; Blackie was going to eat well this morning. I told Catherine to just leave the dishes alone, that I would take care of them later. I took her hand and helped her up from her chair and walked her out onto the front deck. The soft wind that was coming off the river felt good. I could smell the smoke from a fireplace somewhere off in the distance. I held the chair of the picnic table out for her as we sat down in the cool morning breeze. I reached across the table and took both her hands in mine and asked, "Do you want to talk about yesterday?"

She paused for a long time then said, "I saw my mother and father on the television yesterday and things just started flooding back into my mind." She continued, "I remember now some of the things that happened and I got scared all over again." She went on, "There are still bits and pieces that don't make since and it's very frustrating and confusing." She stopped talking and looked down at her lap.

I knew it wasn't easy for her so I said, "Don't try to rush it. Things will come back to you in time, just like they started too yesterday. Just remember that I will be here if you want to talk about anything."

She looked back up at me and smiled. Just then Blackie jumped up at her chair as if to say, "Ok, it's my turn, pay attention to me." Catherine smiled, let go of my hands, put Blackie on her lap and started kissing him.

I had thought about asking Catherine what Popsicle was all about and telling her I had recorded the news show. But I decided to let it go for now. I had told her not to rush things so I figured I shouldn't either. Things would work out in time. We had also planed on leaving today, but under the circumstances it wouldn't hurt to stay a day or two longer. As Catherine and Blackie caught up on the time they had lost together, I excused myself and went to take a shower. After the shower and I had dressed, I felt much better. As I stepped out from the bedroom, Catherine was starting to clean off the table. I stopped her and told her to go back outside and play with the dog. She was hesitant, but I laughingly chased her out and started cleaning up myself. After I was done washing the dishes, I joined her and Blackie on the front deck. We spent the rest of the morning throwing toys for Blackie to chase but didn't say much to each other at all.

The next few days went by fairly quickly. We stayed pretty close to the Pearl with the exception of running up to the marina store for dish soap or toilet paper. Catherine seemed to be withdrawing from me slightly, talking less and that bothered me. The hugs and kisses were slowly turning into quick squeezes and a peck on the lips. The last two nights she slept with her back to me not seeming to want to cuddle. She wasn't talking about anything and I was trying not to force her. I was hoping that she just needed a little more time to get everything straight in her own mind. But those fears I had pushed back in my mind were coming to the front again. I decided it was time to leave Memphis and get us back on what we had come to know as a daily routine, exploring the Mississippi river. It was after one o'clock when we finally shoved off. I knew we wouldn't make it to far before the evening would force us to stop for the night. I was hoping we could find a sandy little beach somewhere and maybe build a campfire to roast some marshmallows as we sat on a blanket. But darkness fell too quickly and we had to drop the anchors just off the bank to spend the night.

Catherine and I had been asleep for a couple of hours when I was awakened by her moaning and tossing. I rolled over and put my hand on her shoulder to try and comfort her. As I did Catherine screamed and sat up shaking and staring at me as if she didn't know me. I looked at her and said, "What's wrong, Sweetheart?"

She just stared at me and started yelling, "Go away! Go away!"

I said, "Catherine, what's wrong?"

She kept staring at me like I was some sort of monster and repeated her demand, "Go away! Just go away!"

I didn't know what to do. I stood up, grabbed my robe, and walked out of the bedroom slamming the bedroom door behind me. I had quit smoking over a month ago but I searched through the kitchen drawers until I found an old pack. I lit a cigarette and walked out onto the front deck. I paced back and forth, puffing rapidly on the cigarette, as I got angrier and angrier. I didn't know what was going on, or how I was suppose to handle the situation, but something had to be done. I decided that tomorrow Catherine and I would have the talk that I had been trying to avoid for fear of causing her more stress. I flipped the still burning tube of tobacco over the railing into the dark murky waters of the river and walked back inside. I stopped and stared at the bedroom door for a minute. I could hear Catherine crying softly. I climbed the latter up to the loft and went back to bed.

The next morning I noticed the bedroom door was open as I climbed down from the loft. Catherine was sitting at the kitchen table with Blackie asleep on her lap. She was still in her pajamas. Her eyes were swollen, and her hair was a mess. She looked like she had been sitting there all night. As I approached her she gently put Blackie on the floor, stood up and softly started crying.

She walked towards me, laid her head against my chest, and wrapped her arms around me. The anger I was feeling last night melted away with her embrace. I put my arms around her and held her tightly. We stood there for a long time; Catherine's tears rolling softly down my bare chest. I kissed the top of her head as I held her, trying to ease her pain. I knew that she didn't understand what was happening to her. But then again, neither did I. After what seemed like an hour, Catherine lifted her head, looked up at me, and still crying said, "I'm sorry."

I gently leaned forward and kissed her forehead. I looked down into her swollen green eyes and softly replied, "You've done nothing to be sorry about." Then I laid my cheek against her head and held her even tighter.

I didn't know how long Catherine had been up, so I slowly walked her back into the bedroom and helped her back into bed. I pulled the covers up over her and gently kissed her forehead. As she slipped off to sleep, I quietly stepped into the bathroom and took a shower. As I finished dressing and stepped back into the bedroom, I could see that Catherine was sleeping peacefully. I left Blackie lying on the bedroom floor to watch over her as I walked out towards the kitchen and closed the door behind me.

It was almost noon and I was sitting at the picnic table on the front deck when Catherine finally emerged from the bedroom still wearing her wrinkled pajamas. I stood up and held a chair out for her as she approached. When she was seated, I went into the kitchen, poured her a glass of milk and took it back to her. As I sat back down I looked across the table at her and asked, "Do you want to talk about last night?"

Holding the glass of milk in both hands and staring at it, she slowly shook her head up and down. I sat quietly waiting for her to begin. I didn't want to rush her or put any more pressure on her than she already felt, but I was anxious to find out what was going on. It took her a few minutes but then she looked up at me and started.

In a low, but clear tone she said, "My name is Catherine Ann Redding. My father is a lawyer named David. My mother's name is Pamela; she's a fifth grade school teacher. I have a younger brother Jesse. It was a Monday morning. I was almost seventeen years old and I was walking to school by myself. My little brother Jesse usually walked with me, but he wasn't feeling good that day and mom kept him home. As I walked down the sidewalk towards the high school I passed an older man standing beside an old torn up van. He looked dirty and was older than my dad. The side door of the van was open and he was standing near the front door pouring something on a rag. I thought he was cleaning the window. As I passed, he grabbed me from behind and shoved the rag over my nose and mouth. I tried to scream and get away but he was too strong and dragged me towards the van. Everything went blank after that. When I woke up, I was tied up and had tape over my mouth. I was in the back of the van and it was moving. I started to scream and tried to get loose. The man pulled the van over, came back to where I was, started hitting me with a stick, and yelling at me to shut up. I was still crying but stopped trying to scream as he went back to the front and started driving again. He kept me tied up and in the van for two days. When we did finally stop, it was dark. He came back, poured that stuff on the rag again, and held it over my face. The next time I woke up it was light out, I was still tied up, and I was in the front of a small motorboat. We were in the swamps. We rode for hours and then came to the shack." Catherine started crying again. I stood up, stepped behind her, and started messaging her shoulders. I reached into my back pocket and handed her my handkerchief.

I looked down at her and said, "Have some of your milk. We can talk some more later."

I left Catherine sitting at the picnic table as she tried to regain her composure and made her some breakfast. Even though it was past noon, I finished cooking the ham and eggs and carried it out to her. As she ate, I thought about what she had said. If she had been seventeen when this guy took her, she was with him a very long time. I also knew that we would have to locate her parents and get her back together with them. The fears in the back of my mind returned. If we were able to find her parents, how would that affect her and I? I was much older than she was. Her family might not care for that. Catherine finished her breakfast and I took her dishes into the kitchen. When I came back outside, I suggested to her that a shower might make her feel better. She excused herself and headed for the bedroom. I sat back down, started to light a cigarette, but then thought about it for a moment and crushed the pack in the palm of my hand. I threw the pack of mangled cigarettes over the railing into the river and waited for Catherine to return.

When Catherine did come back, she looked much better. She was wearing the tan pants outfit. She was smiling and the puffiness around her eyes was gone. Blackie met her half way out on the deck, wagging his tail and panting. She bent down, kissed and rubbed on him, and told him what a pretty puppy he was. For a split second I was actually jealous of the dog. When Catherine was finished loving on Blackie, she walked back over and took her seat again. She sat there for a few minutes then the smile faded away. She looked as if she was trying to get herself angry. If she were mad as she told what happened, then maybe it wouldn't hurt as much.

As I held her hands across the table Catherine picked up from where she had left off. She told me that the first thing the man did when they got to the shack was to drag her up to the bed and rape her. Her lips were curled up and she bit at them as she continued. She explained in gruesome detail how he beat her as he forced himself on her. And how, after he was done, he took the rope off a nail on the wall and tied one end to her leg then the other end to the front porch. He took a blanket off the bed and threw it on the floor next to the cabinet the sink was in. He threw her on the blanket and told her that's where she would sleep. For the next two hours Catherine told the horror story of how she had lived. She told of how she had taken the rope off twice and tried to get away, but there was no place to go. It was all swamps and when he caught her how he beat her until she was almost dead. After the second attempt she never took the rope off again. She explained that when the rope started to rub her leg raw, she would put one foot on top of the other then slip the rope from one ankle to the other ankle without the rope ever coming off her legs. She told of how he never talked except to scream at her to do something and that he would only feed her if there were something left that he didn't want. She said she went days sometimes with out any food. She said he use to beat her for no reason at all with a small whip he had and he raped her on a regular basis. She said, looking back, she was surprised that she had never become pregnant. She thought maybe she couldn't have children or maybe he was sterile. She said she use to dream about her home and family, but after a couple of years the dreams faded away and she forgot all about her earlier life. By the time she had finished I was struggling to hold back my tears. My heart was actually breaking.

I was still holding Catherine's hands in mine. I forced a smile and as I looked into her eyes I said, " Sweetheart, I am so sorry he treated you that way. He's gone now and he will never be able to hurt you again." I let go of her hands, stood up and stepped over to her. I leaned over and kissed the top of her head. She looked up at me and smiled. I walked into the kitchen, wet a cloth, and washed my face. I rinsed out the cloth, grabbed a couple of sodas from the fridge, and re joined Catherine on the front deck. I handed her one of the soft drinks and the cloth. She wiped her face and opened her drink.

As I sat there sipping my soda Catherine started playing with Blackie again. As they played, I told Catherine how I had recorded the news program from the other day. I suggested that we watch it and she could point out her mom and dad to me. In the back of my mind I was hoping it was the Lotto winners. She started smiling and looked pleased that I had recorded it. She stood up and said, "I would love to see them again." I stood up and we headed for the TV.

I turned the TV on and clicked on the "Now playing list". I clicked the news program I had recorded and started fast-forwarding to where she had been watching. Suddenly she started pointing and yelling, "There they are; that's them!" I hit the pause button. I stared at the television in disbelief. I hit the play button and the program started. I increased the volume as I watched Governor David Redding of Minnesota announce his candidacy for President of the United States of America in two thousand eight. Catherine and I turned at the same time and stared at each other with mouths wide open.

My voice almost caught in my throat as I asked, "Your father is the Governor of Minnesota?"

Catherine's shock slowly turned into laughter. "He was a lawyer when I was a kid," she said.

I sat down at the kitchen table and turned the television off. Catherine was still smiling and giggling as she sat down across from me. I looked at Catherine and repeated what I had said, "Your father is the Governor of the State of Minnesota!" Catherine stopped giggling but didn't say anything. I had to think about this. I needed some time to digest everything that was happening. I walked back out onto the front deck.

Catherine seemed to sense my concerns and followed me out. As she took a seat she asked, "Is everything all right?" As I paced around the deck, I looked over at her and said, "Yeah, everything's fine. But it might be complicated."

Catherine looked confused as she asked, "How so?"

I stopped pacing and sat down. I said, "Well, your dad is a Governor and you can't just pick up a phone and call him. He would have secretaries that field his calls. They would want to know what we were calling about. I'm not sure that letting someone other than your parents know about this would be wise. If it should leak out to the press that you're alive and well it could be a nightmare for you before you even got to see your parents."

Catherine's face turned white. Her eyes opened wide. She looked startled. She placed her hand over her mouth and looked from side to side as if she was looking for some place to run. She suddenly stood up and bolted towards the bedroom and started to cry. I jumped up and ran after her. As I caught up to her she was sitting on the edge of the bed. I took her shoulders in my hands and asked, " Are you all right? Did I say something that upset you?"

Catherine lowered her hands from her mouth, looked up at me with watery green eyes, and said, "I hadn't thought about getting to see my parents again. What if they don't want to see me? What if they're mad at me? What if they don't like me anymore?"

I started smiling, but my heart was breaking for her again. I kneeled down on one knee and looked up at her. I said, "Of course your parents still love you. And I'm sure that there's nothing in the world that would make them happier than to see you again."

Catherine looked at me with tears still streaming down her cheeks and asked, "Are you sure?"

Still looking up at her I smiled and said, "I've never been more sure of anything in my life."

Catherine was having a rough time of it. The last few days had been taking its toll on her emotions. They had been wreaking havoc on mine as well. She seemed to be calming down again so I suggested that we go do some investigating on the computer. I helped her up and we walked back into the kitchen. I sat her down and turned on the PC. When it finally came on I went to Google and typed in Governor, Minnesota. It pulled up a number of queries, one of which was the Wikipedia of the Current

Governor of Minnesota. I clicked on that one. I started reading out loud about Governor David Preston Redding. He was born in nineteen forty-four in St. Paul, Minnesota. He went to Harvard law school where he met his wife Pamela Ann Harrington. After college, David and his wife came back to St Paul were he started what became a very successful law firm, Redding and Associates. David was elected Governor in nineteen ninety-eight and again in two thousand four. The Redding's had three children. Catherine Ann Redding, born May 2nd, 1972. Jesse Cody Redding, born January 12th, 1974. And Alicia Catherine Redding, born June 6th, 1991.

I stopped reading and looked over at Catherine and said, "You have a little sister and she's named after you." Catherine stared at the screen and put her hands over her mouth as her eyes filled with tears of joy. She looked over at me crying and smiling at the same time. I continued reading. It went on to tell about how Catherine disappeared on May 1st 1989, just one day before her seventeenth birthday. It said that the police never did discover what had happened to her. There were no ransom demands and a body was never found. It was as if she just disappeared off the face of the planet with out a trace. The biography went on to tell about Catherine's brother Jesse. He had followed in his father's shoes, had gone on to Harvard, and became a lawyer himself. He was now the District Attorney in St. Paul. It told of her younger sister Alicia and how she was enrolled in a very exclusive private school for girls only. As I came to the end of the web page, Catherine was slobbering all over the place. I handed her my handkerchief again. She was crying with joy over hearing something about her family and the sister she never knew.

I went back to Google and typed in David Preston Redding. Again there were a lot of queries found. I looked until I saw the Governors own website. I clicked on it and found lots of pictures of the entire family. Catherine really started pouring the tears out.

She was laughing, crying and pointing as we went from one picture to the next. There were family and individual pictures; we studied them all. At the bottom of the website, there was a large picture of Catherine when she was about sixteen with a caption beneath it that read, "In loving memory" I started crying.

I shut off the computer and Catherine and I sat there laughing with tears running down both our faces. I grabbed us a couple more drinks from the fridge and sat back down. As the laughter started to subside, I asked Catherine, "What was all that talk about Popsicle the other day?"

She got a big smile on her face and shyly said, "When I was in the third or forth grade, a kid at school called his dad pop. I thought it sounded cute so when I got home I called my dad pop. He wasn't too thrilled with that title so I told him I was going to call him Popsicle instead. He liked that much better and from then on that's what I called him."

I looked over at Catherine and said, "Looks like we're heading to St. Paul."

Catherine just smiled and said, "Ok."

Chapter 9

It was late in the afternoon and I knew we wouldn't get to far, but I raised the anchors, fired up the engine, and started up the river. It was almost a thousand miles from where we were to St. Paul. Figuring eight miles an hour and twelve hours a day, I figured it would take us ten days to get there. That was not counting what little we would do today. I glanced at my cell phone. It was April 22nd. Using my fingers I figured out that it would put us there---------on May 2nd. That was Catherine's birthday. She would turn thirty-five. I thought to myself that was only fitting. It would be a great birthday present for all. It also occurred to me that Catherine would have been away for eighteen years and one day. Eighteen years tied to that rope. I literally shook as a cold chill passed over me.

Catherine had me put the pictures of her family back on the computer. She was scrolling down the web page studying them as I drove. It was getting late. The sun would be down in another hour or less. I looked over at Catherine and thought how pretty she really was. Before I even realized that I was talking, the words came rushing out of my mouth as I asked, "Sweetheart, will you marry me?"

Catherine stopped looking at the pictures and looked very shocked as she responded, "What?"

I said, "You and me! Lets get married." There was a very long pause then I said, "Are we still a couple?"

As her head started to drop and the smile left her face, I knew what the answer was before she even replied. She said, "I don't know. I don't know what I'm supposed to feel or think." She looked back up at me and continued, "It's not you. You're the best thing that has ever happened to me. You're the only person in the world I can trust. It's just that everything is so confusing to me right now."

I forced a smile on my face and then turned back to driving the Pearl. I was loosing her and I knew it. The fears in the back of my mind didn't just come forward again. They were realized.

The next ten days went by very slowly. I was sleeping in the loft again and Catherine and I seemed to be dancing around each other's feelings. It sadly reminded me of when my wife and mine's marriage started to fall apart twenty years ago. We both knew something was wrong, but we didn't know how to talk about it. She tried, but I was too damn stubborn to admit that there was a problem, so we said nothing too each other and slowly started drifting apart just like Catherine and I were doing now. It had gotten so bad that my wife started confiding in a friend at work. She found that she could talk to him and since I wasn't talking to her, a romance developed between the two of them. When the marriage finally did come to an end and I found out about him, I accused her of betrayal and blamed him for stealing my wife. I hated them both for years, but then realized it was my own damn fault for not being there for her when things were not going along as smoothly as they had when we first got married. I was doing the same thing all over again. I knew I should be talking to Catherine, but I didn't know how. I knew I should be fighting as hard as I could to save the one thing that made me feel whole again after all these years. I really didn't know how. I knew that I could have fought the biker back in Natchez until one of us was dead, but I had no idea how to fight for Catherine. Every time I tried to say something to her, about the two of us, or how I felt about her, my words came out all wrong and I wound up feeling I looked like a fool. I found myself saying nothing again, knowing in my heart where that would lead. I have never been afraid of anything or anyone in my life, but the thought of loosing Catherine, and not knowing how to stop it, scared the hell out of me. Catherine and I shared the driving between us as we made our way up the river. We made good time every day, but the closeness that had grown between us was fading rapidly. I started feeling that we couldn't get to St. Paul soon enough. If the axe was going to fall, I just wanted it over with quickly.

It was about four-thirty in the afternoon when we pulled into St. Paul. I found a marina and slipped the Pearl up next to the dock. As I jumped onto the dock to tie the mooring lines off, I noticed two men holding hands and walking towards me. They were both as bald as a cucumber and both had mustaches. The thinner of the two had a large handlebar mustache. As they approached I stood up after tying down the rear line.

The thinner of the two said, "Hi there. My name is Tim and this is Troy, we're the proprietors of this lovely marina."

As I extended my hand I said, "Glad to meet you."

Tim shook my hand first, then Troy. Tim continued, "We just had to come down, introduce ourselves and look at this lovely boat of yours."

Troy had walked towards the rear of the Pearl and yelled, "Oh look Tim; it's named The Black Pearl."

Tim responded, "That's so cute. I just love Johnny Depp and the little pirate flag up there is so adorable."

Troy walked back over and as he took Tim's hand again he looked at me and asked, "Is it for sale? Oh, please, say yes!"

I looked at the two of them as they cuddled close together and said, "Sorry guys, she's not for sale, but if I ever do decide to let her go, I'll keep you in mind." I told Tim and Troy that I would be up later this evening to settle up with them on mooring charges and probably pick up a few supplies.

Troy said, "Make it about seven and you can join us for strawberry daiquiris, it's daiquiri night. We all ways have daiquiris on Tuesdays."

Tim added, "Troy simply makes the most scrumptious daiquiris you've ever tasted."

Troy smiled and looked embarrassed then playfully hit Tim on his shoulder.

I said, "I'll try." Then I jumped back on the Pearl and walked into the cabin. Catherine was sitting at the kitchen table as I walked in. She looked sad. I looked at her and said, "We had better hurry if we're going to get out of here in time to catch your parents."

She looked up at me and said, "I can't go."

I stopped in my tracks. I said, "What do you mean you can't go? We just traveled for ten days to get here. It's your birthday. Seeing your parents will be a great birthday present for you and them."

Catherine started to cry. With her eyes filling with water she said, "I'm afraid."

I tried to control my emotions. I wasn't angry, just confused, and I didn't want her to hear it in my voice. As calmly as I could I said, "Afraid of what Sweetheart?"

The tears were coming down hard now as she said, "I don't know. I'm just afraid. What if they won't see me? What if they don't want me? I'm just afraid!"

I kneeled down next to her and took her hand. There was no way I could force her to go, so I said, "Ok Sweetheart, if you feel that strongly about it, I'll go. If you're right and they don't want to see you, I will be coming back by myself and we will deal with that then. If I'm right and they love you just half as much as I do, they will be with me when I return."

She slowed her crying and looked at me and said, "Ok."

I stood up and walked into the bedroom to get ready. It was getting close to five-thirty by the time I finished getting dressed. I was tying my tie as I entered the living room. Catherine had Blackie in her lap petting him. I leaned over, kissed Catherine on the top of her head, and told Blackie to keep an eye on her for me. I told them both, I would be back in an hour or so and walked out the door. I stopped at the marina store and asked Tim and Troy for a phone book. I called a cab and settled up with Tim for the mooring charges as I waited. The cab arrived quickly and I headed off.

As the driver pulled away, I pulled the address I had gotten off Google out of my pocket and said, "1006 Summit Avenue, please."

The cabbie turned and looked at me and asked, "You going to see the Governor?"

I laughed and answered, "Yes, I hope so." It was only a ten-minute trip. I paid the driver and thanked him as I got out. The house was fantastic. No wonder they call it a mansion. I walked up to the gate and pressed the button on the speaker.

A few seconds later a female voice came over and said, "Can I help you?"

I replied, "Yes I need to talk to Governor Redding, please."

The voice came back and said, "And what would this be concerning, may I ask?"

I answered, "It's of a personal matter."

There was a short pause and the voice said, "You will need to make an appointment to see the Governor tomorrow at the capital building."

I thought for a second then I said, "Do me just one favor. Go give the Governor one word for me. Popsicle."

The pause was much longer this time. When the voice came back, I heard the electronic switch on the gate trip. The voice said, "Please walk to the front door."

As I pushed the gate closed behind me and walked up the long walkway to the front door, a very large man in a suit and tie with a very big gun met me. The gentleman stopped me and ran his hands up and down my person, searching for a weapon. When he was satisfied I had none, he escorted me to the front door. When we arrived at the door, it opened and a sweet looking little old lady asked me to follow her. The gentleman that was with me and I followed her. She lead us to what appeared to be a library and she asked me to wait. My newfound friend stood silently next to the door and never took his eyes off of me. I had never seen a place as elegant as this. I had been a general contractor for thirty years and had seen some of the finest homes there were, but this place made them all look like shacks. I was looking at the solid oak paneling when the door opened and Governor Redding walked in. He didn't waist a second as he walked over to me and said, "You have two minutes to convince me not to have Alex here break both your legs then call the police and have you thrown in jail. I have a fundraiser I have to leave for and I'm not going to be late." I started to tell him why I was there when he cut me off and continued, "Your not the first son-of-a-bitch that has come to me about my daughter with some kind of story they think will get them a lot of money." He went on, "But you are the first one to know something that no one else has." He demanded, "Where did you hear about Popsicle?"

He finally stopped talking. I quickly answered, "Catherine told me about how when she was in the third or forth grade she started calling you that."

The Governor almost screamed, "Catherine told you that, huh? And just when did she tell you this?"

I answered again quickly, "Just a few days ago when we started up to see you." The Governor started to say something but I cut him off this time. I said, "Governor Redding, I'm not here to blow smoke up your skirt or try and get any money from you. If you give me just five minutes, I'm sure you will cancel your dinner appointment and this will become one of the happiest days of your life."

The Governor looked over at Alex. Alex just shrugged his shoulders. The Governor looked back at me and said, "Ok, you now have five minutes before Alex kills you."

I smiled nervously I'm sure and said, "What I need to tell you would best be accomplished if your wife were here."

The Governor thought for a second then motioned for Alex to go get her. Alex was only gone a few moments when he and the First Lady walked back in. I asked the Governor if we might sit down. The Governor pointed to a chair and I took a seat. He and the First Lady sat on the couch across from me. They both looked at me and waited for me to start talking.

I started telling them the whole story of how I got lost back in February and found this woman somewhere back in the swamps of Louisiana. How she was tied to a rope, starving and afraid, and didn't know anything. Who she was or how she got there. I told them of how I searched for a place that would take her and help her and how there were no places like that to be found. As I continued I told them how we lived on the Pearl and how I had bought her a dog. I told them about her fear of men and what had happened in the bar that night in Mississippi.

I was about to go on when the First Lady spoke up. She asked, "Are you telling me that Cathy is alive?"

I laughed and said, "I mean no disrespect Mrs. Redding, but Catherine told me she would kill anyone who called her Cathy or Katie. She hates those names."

The First Lady looked over at the Governor and said, "He's right."

The Governor was getting impatient. He stood up and yelled, "Look I've had just about enough of this story. Either tell us where Catherine is, or I'll have you thrown in jail."

I looked up at the Governor and said, "Governor Redding, you can do that if you choose to, but it will just delay your seeing your daughter until I am sure you understand everything Catherine has been through." I continued, "I know it must be difficult for you and the First Lady after all this time, but Catherine was tied to that rope for eighteen years. Her back is ripped to pieces from all the beatings she got. She was raped repeatedly. Until I know that you understand all of this, I'm not going to let you, or anyone else, rush down there and make things worse for her. I care a great deal for your daughter and I promised her I wouldn't let anyone hurt her ever again." The Governor sat back down. I went on. I told them of how Catherine saw both he and the First Lady on CNN when he announced his run for The Oval Office thirteen days ago and how it sparked her to start remembering things again. Then I finished by telling them how Catherine was afraid to come here tonight. How she was afraid that her own mother and father would be mad at her or not want her anymore. The first lady started to cry. I added, "Today is Catherine's birthday, I can't think of a better gift for her than to get her family back."

The Governor said, "Ok, I only have one question left. How do we know that you're not like all the rest, and have some woman that looks like Catherine that has studied our lives, and knows how to act the part?"

I smiled and answered him, "First of all I am not asking for anything, except for Catherine's happiness. Two; there's always DNA and fingerprints. I'm sure that as Governor you can have that checked out in a matter of hours, if not minutes." Everything became eerily quiet. Finally I said, "Ok, if you are sure you can approach Catherine, knowing all that she's been through and take it slow, we can go get her."

The Governor and the First Lady looked at each other with anticipation and started to stand. The Governor looked over at Alex and said, "Tell Rosie to cancel all my appointments tonight, then come back; you're going with us."

As we walked towards the garage, I was convinced in my mind that the only reason Alex was going along was to shoot me if I was lying. As we entered the garage I saw this long black limonene. I thought to myself, not too conspicuous. Alex held the door as we all piled in. The Governor asked, "Where to?"

I replied, "The Third Street Marina." The Governor picked up the phone and gave the driver the directions. The ten-minute drive was made in complete silence. As we got to the marina and started walking towards the Pearl, I could see Tim and Troy staring out the window of the marina store. They followed our every move all the way down to the Pearl.

As we stepped up onto the front deck, I held open the sliding glass doors and let the First Lady and the Governor in. Alex stayed out on the deck. Catherine was not in the living room. I excused myself and went to the bedroom door. I knocked softly. There was no reply. I opened the door and entered, closing the door behind me. Catherine was sitting on the bed holding Blackie. I looked down at her and asked, "Are you all right?" She just shook her head up and down. I smiled and said, "I told you they would come." Catherine stared at the bedroom door. I continued, "They're here because they love you and missed you and they're dying to see you." Catherine still didn't say anything; she just looked up at me with uncertainty on her face. I took Catherine's hands in mine and said, "You're parents are right outside. You've waited a long time to see them again. Everything is ok, I'll be right there beside you."

Catherine asked, "Will you?" I smiled and shook my head up and down. I put Blackie on the floor and helped Catherine to her feet. I put my arm around her shoulders and opened the bedroom door. As we stepped out into the living room the First Lady caught her breath and held her hands up over her mouth. The Governor's eyes began to water. There would be no DNA tests or fingerprints taken. They knew instantly this was Catherine.

Catherine and I paused at the door for just a moment, Catherine screamed, "Momma;" and bolted from my arms. Catherine and the First Lady locked into an unbreakable embrace.

The Governor wrapped his arms around both of them. They were all three crying hysterically.

I left the three of them standing and crying in each other's arms, went to my drawer, and took out three handkerchiefs. As I approached them and started handing out the pieces of cloth, they all looked up and started laughing. They took the handkerchiefs and started blotting at their eyes. As I stood there watching the three of them I knew that Catherine was really home now. Her life would be one of love, not torture. I looked at Catherine's smiling face and said to myself, "Happy birthday Sweetheart."

I let the festivities go on for a few more minutes, but the living room was way too small for this party so I suggested we move out onto the deck where we would all be more comfortable. As we walked out I happen to look over at Alex. He smiled at me and gave me thumbs up. I smiled back in appreciation and was happy just to know he wasn't going to shoot me.

The Governor and First Lady had obviously been paying attention back at the mansion. They were great. They never asked Catherine a single question. They only told her how pretty she was and how much they had missed her. They told her all about the family, how her brother was doing, and everything about her little sister. They must have told her a hundred times how much they loved her. To me, that was exactly what I felt she needed. I was dying to tell her the same thing, but I kept my mouth shut. Blackie was running around jumping up at everyone, trying to get some attention of his own. It was a festive mood, however bittersweet for me.

Even though the Governor and the First Lady didn't seem to be in any rush to leave, after about forty-five minutes into the reunion on the deck, the Governor suggested that we all head back to the mansion so Catherine could meet her little sister. He took out his cell phone and dialed. A second later we all heard him say, "Hey son, I don't know what your involved in but drop what ever it is and come over to the house." There was a pause then the Governor continued, "I didn't go to the fundraiser. Something else came up that was much more important." The Governor was smiling from ear to ear. "Just drop what you're doing and meet us at the house. I will explain when you get there." He hung up, looked at us and said, "Shall we go?"

As the five of us walked up towards the limousine with Blackie in tow, I could see Tim and Troy peering out the marina store window again. Just then the movement of someone hiding in the bushes next to the store caught my attention. He was taking pictures. Working the camera as fast as he could. I knew that the story would soon be out, but at least Catherine was with her family now and the Governor could protect her from the paparazzi. I laughed to myself and thought, let them mess with Alex.

When we got back to the mansion, I could see the astonishment in Catherine's eyes as she walked through the house with all it's marble and oak. It was a far cry from the shack she had lived in for so many years. The First Lady excused herself as soon as we walked in and the rest of us were lead into the library once more. The Governor remarked, "This calls for a celebration" and opened a bottle of very expensive cognac. He poured himself, Alex and I a drink. Then he pulled out a humidor and offered us a cigar. As I took the long cylindrical object from the box, I noticed that it was a Cohiba and that it had a black and yellow band but no red dot. I looked up at the Governor with suspicion in my eyes and he just smiled as he lit his and handed me a solid gold cigar clipper. I would probably be thrown in jail for the rest of my life if I had just one of these. He had a humidor full of them and was flaunting it. It must be nice to be a Governor I thought to myself. I lit the cigar and took a sip of the cognac. Yes, it is very nice to be a Governor.

The First Lady returned a few seconds later, arm in arm with Alicia, Catherine's younger sister. Alicia was sixteen and looked like a young Grace Kelley stepping out of the castle in Monaco. The First Lady looked at Alicia and said, "Alicia, this is your sister Catherine." Catherine just stood there not knowing what to do.

Alicia smiled, walked over to Catherine, put her arms around her, and hugged her tightly as she said, "Hi Catherine, it's nice to finally meet you."

Catherine held her sister as she started to cry and said, "You're so beautiful." After a few minutes of hugging and wiping back tears, we all sat down on the couches to get acquainted. That is everyone except Alex. He just stood at the doorway sipping his cognac, puffing on his Cuban cigar, and smiling as he watched over us all.

Catherine and Alicia were inseparable. They sat on the couch holding on to each other tightly. We were all laughing and listening to the First Lady telling Catherine all about Alicia and all the boys that were courting her. Just then the maid stepped into the library and told the Governor that his son was here. The Governor stood up and walked towards the front of the house. A few minutes later he returned with Jesse and his wife. It became apparent that the Governor had not told him about Catherine. As the three of them walked into the library, Jesse looked over and saw Catherine sitting on the couch next to Alicia. He stopped and stared for a long moment. Catherine stood up, tears again forming in her eyes. Finally Jesse asked in a low voice, "Catherine?" Then he yelled, "Oh my God, Catherine!" And he bolted towards her. As Jesse and Catherine embraced, Jesse almost collapsed in her arms. They were both crying, but Jesse was almost inconsolable. The Governor had to walk over and help hold him up as he clung to Catherine. Jesse was almost hysterical as his emotions poured out like a bursting dam. He started screaming, "I'm sorry, I'm so sorry." Finally the Governor had to pry Jesse away from Catherine and sat him down in a chair. Jesse's wife ran over to try and comfort him. Catherine kneeled down at his chair and held his hand. Jesse just couldn't stop crying. As he held his face in the palms of his hands, he just kept repeating, "I'm sorry." The Governor brought over a handkerchief and a glass of water. Jesse's wife took them and tried to help Jesse calm down. We all stood in silence as we watched the young man attempt to deal with his pain.

It took about thirty minutes, but Jesse finally started to calm down a little. The Governor brought Jesse's wife a couple of sedatives and told her that she and Jesse should plan on staying here tonight. Catherine was confused about how Jesse was reacting to seeing her again. It showed in her eyes as she looked up at her mother. The First Lady gently reached down and pulled Catherine up. She walked her over to where the Governor, Alicia and I were standing. The first lady looked sadly into Catherine's eyes and said, "You're brother has always blamed himself for not walking you to school that day."

Catherine stared at her mother for a second then pulled away from her and kneeled back down at Jesse's chair. As she took his hands in hers again, she looked up into his still swollen eyes and softly said, "It's not your fault. There's nothing you could have done. I'm back now and I've missed you and I love you very much."

The sedatives were starting to work on Jesse now. He was no longer crying but he appeared to be very tired and was very lethargic. As Catherine let go of his hands and stood up, the Governor and Jesse's wife helped him up to their room for the night. It had been a very emotional homecoming for Catherine to say the least. When the Governor returned, Alicia was sitting on the couch playing with Blackie. The First Lady and Catherine were huddled together talking on the other one. Alex was still standing guard at the door. I met the Governor as he walked half way into the room. I thanked him for his hospitality and the Cuban cigar and told him that I should be getting back to the

Pearl. The Governor said, "Nonsense, stay here tonight, we have plenty of room."

I smiled and thanked him again for his offer but told him that tonight was a time for his wife and he to get to know their daughter again and I wasn't part of that. I asked if I could just call a cab, I would be leaving. Catherine obviously had over heard our conversation.

With the First Lady in tow she walked up to me and asked, "You're not leaving, are you?" Without waiting for a reply she continued, "You can't leave!" She looked up at the Governor and said, "Make him stay he can't go!"

I smiled at her and repeated what I had told her father. I said, "Sweetheart, you don't need me any more. You're back home now with you're family. You need time to get to know each other all over again. I would just be in the way." I pulled out my wallet, took out an old business card, and wrote my cell phone number on the back of it. I handed the card to Catherine and continued, "This is my cell phone number. You can reach me on it night or day if you ever need me." I stared into her sparkling green eyes one last time and gently leaned over and kissed her forehead. I looked over at the Governor and asked, "The cab?"

The Governor looked at Catherine then back at me and said, "I'll have my driver take you." I handed the First Lady the tube of cream I had brought with me for Catherine's back and turned to go with the Governor. Alex smiled and tipped his head at me as the Governor and I started walking towards the garage.

As we entered the garage, the Governor picked up the receiver from the phone on the wall and called for his driver. As we waited he looked at me and said, "Terry, you're a good man. You know that there was a very sizable reward offered on Catherine's behalf many years ago. You're entitled to it."

I looked down at the floor of the garage and put my hand up like I was scratching my forehead. I didn't want the Governor to see the water building up in my eyes. I said, "Governor Redding,

I've already had my reward. It was having known you're daughter for these past few months." As the driver entered the garage, the Governor patted me on the shoulder and opened the limousine door. As I stepped into the limo, I looked back at the Governor and said, "Take good care of Catherine." I rode back to the marina, alone in the back of that extremely large limousine and it only served to multiply the emptiness welling up inside of me. Even Blackie was gone. I was alone again.

As I arrived back at the marina and stepped from the limo, I saw Tim and Troy running towards me from the store. They were both out of breath as they slid to a stop in front of me. After a few seconds of catching their breath, Tim finally asked, "Was that the Governor and his wife we saw you with earlier?" Troy put his arm around Tim's waste and laid his head on his shoulder, still looking at me and trying to breath, as they both waited on my response. I shook my head up and down. Tim looked at Troy and said, "See, I told you it was the Governor. I know what the Governor looks like."

Troy raised his head and asked, "Do you know the Governor personally?"

I smiled at the two of them and said, "No, I just met him for the first time tonight."

Tim chimed in, "How did you meet him? What's he like? Is the First Lady as glorious as they say she is?"

I laughed at the two of them. They were funny. They had picked my spirits up considerably in just the short time I had arrived back at the marina. I started patting my pockets, looking for a cigarette, but of course I knew I didn't have any. I asked, "Do either of you smoke?" Troy quickly pulled a pack of Marlboro from his shirt pocket and offered me one. I took the cigarette and leaned forward as Troy held up the burning lighter for me. I almost chocked as I took the first drag. It had been a long time since my last one. I looked over at the two of them and said, "Look, do you guys like Parrot Bay Rum?"

Troy spoke up and said, "Tim can drink it straight with a soda back, but I have to mix it. It's just to strong for me." Tim puffed his chest out and smiled.

I said, "Ok, I have a full bottle of rum and all the soda we need. Come on down to the Pearl and I will tell you the whole story."

Tim looked at Troy and said, "Did you hear that? The Pearl! That's so cute." As we started walking down the dock, Tim and Troy was locked arm in arm. Suddenly, Tim reached over, grabbed my arm, and said, "Look the three amigos." Troy didn't seemed to be amused and I was quite sure that they were going to have a few words about it later. We continued our trip down the dock towards my boat.

Tim and Troy sat out on the front deck of the boat at the picnic table. It was dark and the light breeze blowing off the Mississippi felt good. There was a heavy damp smell to the air. I flipped on the deck lights as I walked into the kitchen to get our drinks. I filled three tall glasses with ice and poured them three quarters full of rum. I filled the ice chest full of soda and put Jimmy Buffet on the CD player. I carried the drinks and ice chest out to the table. Tim and Troy sat close together on the other side waiting in anticipation for my story. I bummed another cigarette from Troy, passed out the drinks, and began to tell them both how I came to buy the Pearl and set off on my adventure. For the next hour and a half I explained in great detail what had happened from the day I took possession until tonight. As I spoke, they both listened intently. When I got to the part about the biker in the bar, Troy, half drunk, popped up and said, "I bet you would have killed that great big bully." Tim looked at Troy and shook his head up and down in agreement.

As I continued, I told them about the two weeks on the sandy beach. Tim breathed a heavy sigh and said, "That's so sweet." As I finished my story and told them of what happened in the Governors mansion tonight, Troy started softly crying and blowing his nose into his handkerchief. I noticed that the bottle of rum was almost empty. Troy was plastered and the soft crying was slowly turning into a full-scale flood now. Tim wasn't in much better shape. Tim looked up at me and said, "You poor thing you," as he patted Troy on the back trying to console him. Tim, still looking at me and weaving back and forth in his chair, said, "Catherine sounds like such a sweet girl."

By the looks of the two of them I knew it was time for this party to end. I lit another cigarette from the pack that Troy had given me. I told Tim I would be leaving in the morning. I helped him get Troy to his feet and walked them both over to the dock. I watched as the two of them staggered up towards the store. It wasn't clear to me which one was holding the other up. I was afraid that they might walk off the side and wind up in the river. I kept an eye on them until they reached the front door of the store. I flipped the cigarette over the dock into the black murky water, walked inside the cabin, locked up and headed to bed. I laid my phone on the nightstand so I could hear it if it rang. It never did.

Chapter 10

The next morning I woke up just as the sun was starting to rise. As I swung my legs over the side of the bed and sat up, I had to grab the sides of my head in an attempt to stop the pounding headache. I made a mental note not to buy any more rum. I slowly walked into the kitchen and grabbed a soda from the fridge. The houseboat seemed eerily quiet. As I stood there by the kitchen table in my briefs, I took a large gulp of the pop and flipped open the atlas that was lying on the kitchen table. As I studied the maps, I lit a cigarette and continued to down the sweet tasting soda. I noticed that about twenty miles south of where I was now the river forked and headed north where it joined a number of nice looking lakes. As I took the last swallow of soda, I decided that would be a good place to start as I made my way back down the Mississippi. I dropped the cigarette into the empty soda can, tossed it into the trashcan, and headed for the shower.

When I had finished my shower and dressed, I stepped out the rear door of the bedroom into the back yard. The warmth of the sun felt good on my face. I scanned the grassy deck but saw no morning gifts left behind by Blackie that needed to be cleaned up. As I surveyed the small back yard I noticed that the little four-foot tree was now taller than I was. Its leaves were bright green and its branches were spreading out nicely. As a seagull flew overhead and screeched good morning, I focused my attention back on getting ready to shove off. I stepped down onto the deck and untied the rear mooring line. I gave the rear of the Pearl a little shove then walked to the front to untie that line. As I jumped back onto the front deck to get underway, I saw Tim and Troy standing on the porch of the store waving. I turned around, faced them and waved goodbye.

As I turned the key on the helm, the engine came to life. The Pearl seemed to want to leave as badly as I did. I backed her out, turned her around, and headed south. I sat the atlas in front of me so I could study it a little more as I started my trip back down the river. I flipped on the CD player, lit the last cigarette in the pack that Troy had given me, and was happy I had started the voyage. Going down the river with the current was much faster than it had been going against it on our way up. I should be able to make good time and get out of St. Paul quickly. The Pearl seemed to agree as she hummed along and sliced through the murky water. She needed fuel and I could use a few supplies, but I knew we had more than enough to make it to Prescott where we would turn north and head up to the lakes, so I decided I would get it all there. I just wanted out of St. Paul.

It was almost nine when I carefully guided the Pearl up to the pumps in Prescott. As I tied her off I asked the attendant to fill her up with fuel and water and pump out the sewage. Then I headed up to the store to get my supplies. As I was walking through the small store, picking up toilet paper and potato chips, I heard the television that the young lady behind the counter was watching. The news reporter was saying something about the Governor. I walked over and joined her at the counter. She was watching CNN and Wolf was talking about how the Governor of Minnesota had missed his first fundraiser last night. Wolf was smiling and almost making fun of the Governor saying that this was the first time someone who was running for the White House didn't even bother to show up and take the money that people wanted to throw at him. Wolf continued with, "But we do have pictures of the Governor and the First Lady last night walking up a dock somewhere in St. Paul with three other people." The pictures were obviously from the guy at the marina last night showing us walking up the dock and getting into the limousine. Wolf added, "They all seemed to be laughing and having a good time. I just hope it was worth the two million dollars he didn't get at the fundraiser." He went on, "The Governor will be holding a press conference at eleven o'clock this morning and we will be bringing that to you live when it happens." I finished up my shopping, bought a carton of cigarettes, and headed back to the Pearl.

When I pulled away from the dock, I crossed the river and headed up the fork that would take me to the lakes. The Pearl was fighting the current once more and the banks of the river passed by a lot slower. I had seen a marina on the atlas just north of Stillwater that I figured I could get to before two o'clock this afternoon. I was in no hurry and that seemed like a good place to stop. I would still have plenty of daylight left and I might even get in some fishing. I was trying to keep my mind on driving and fishing, or anything other than Catherine. But every song on the CD player reminded me of her in one-way or another. If I turned it off the silence would just reminded me that she and Blackie were not here.

It was about one o'clock. According to the atlas and my speed I figured I was about a half hour away from the marina. I was just about to light another cigarette when my cell phone started ringing. I almost dropped it as I tried to pull it out of my shirt pocket. My fingers didn't want to cooperate as I tried to push the small button to answer it. I finally got the phone up to my ear and said, "Hello!"

My heart sank as the male voice on the other end said, "Terry, this is Detective Rogers in New Orleans."

I felt like all the air had just been sucked out of me and my voice almost cracked as I responded, "Hey Charlie, what's up?"

Charlie said, "I just saw your picture on TV. Was that really Governor Redding's daughter you had on the boat with you down here?"

I paused for a long time then answered, "Yeah, her name is Catherine."

Charlie replied, "Man, it's all over the news. Everyone's trying to find out who the mystery man is that saved her. You're a hero. A celebrity."

I paused again then said, "Charlie, I'm not a hero and I certainly don't want to be a celebrity." I added, "Catherine is home now with her family. It wouldn't be a big story if we had found out her parents lived in a trailer park somewhere. Please do me a favor. You're the only one who knows my last name other than Catherine. Please don't tell anyone who I am and please don't let anyone get their hands on your report." I continued in a not so friendly tone, "I bet if anyone had known who she was when I was down there, people would have broken their backs to get me the help I had begged for."

Charlie paused this time then finally said, "You're right. We didn't help you very much when you were here. I'm sorry that life is the way it is. She's home now, that's the important thing. I'm proud to know you. I'm proud of what you did. Trust me, I won't say a word about this to anyone."

As I calmed down and regained a little friendlier composure I said, "Thank you, Charlie."

Charlie replied, "If you ever make it back down this way again, the drinks are on me."

As I hung up I could see the marina up ahead. It would feel good to stop.

Once the Pearl was all tied down and secured for the night, I walked up to the marina store. There was an older gentleman behind the counter that took care of the mooring charges and a carton of worms for me. We got to talking and I asked, "Where could a guy find some good fishing around here"

He laughed and said, "About the only place you couldn't catch a nice size fish was if you were fishing in the bathroom sink." Then he added, "And you might just get one there too." He did admit that the farther north I went the bigger the fish were, but then said, "If you throw a line off the end of the pier out there you'll be happy with what you get." As I started to leave the store, the old man yelled out to me, "Did you hear about them finding the Governor's daughter?" I stopped and looked back and shook my head up and down. He said, "Can you imagine that, after all these years?" I just smiled at him and headed back down to the boat.

As I stepped up on the front deck of the Pearl, I picked out a good rod and reel and entered the cabin. I put John Denver on the CD player and turned on the speakers to the back deck. I grabbed some cigarettes, a six-pack of beer, and walked out to the back yard. I raised the umbrella, sat the beer and the cigarettes on the picnic table, and took a seat. As I baited my hook and cast it out, I thought to myself, if I had to be miserable I could at least do it with class and get drunk singing about it with an old friend. I lit a cigarette, opened a beer and thought to myself that I was getting back into my old habits. I was drinking and smoking as much as I ever had and it had only taken me a day to get back into it. As I watched an eagle flying above the trees on the other side of the river, John sang about the Colorado countryside. I looked out at the tall green trees on the distant bank. With the eagle flying high over the sparkling clear water in front of me, I felt like he was sitting next to me, singing about this place.

The old man at the store was right, the fishing here was great. I caught some very nice size bass and one very large channel cat. I was more into feeling sorry for myself, and drinking and singing, than I was into cleaning fish, so I threw them back each time I caught one. Depression and not eating allowed the miracles of the golden liquid that I was drinking to do its job. The CD ended about the same time the six-pack did. I reeled in my line and stood the pole up against the railing, crushed out my cigarette, and walked back into the bedroom to take a nap. Maybe sleep would let my mind forget about Catherine for just a little while if I were lucky.

When I woke up it was already dark. I looked at the clock and it said eight thirty five. I had slept for almost five hours. I felt great. I felt as if the chalkboard had been wiped clean and the writing was starting all over again fresh. I walked into the bathroom and took a hot shower. As I slipped into clean clothes, I thought I would walk up to the bar I had seen when I was at the store. A night out would do me good. Who knows, I might even get lucky tonight. I combed my hair, splashed on some aftershave, slipped my wallet into my back pocket, and headed out.

As I entered the bar, the music was loud and the place was packed. There was a large banner on the wall that read Karaoke every Wednesday night. There was a young lady on the stage singing very badly. The music was too loud for the song she was attempting and she was screaming the lyrics trying to match the music. It didn't help. And it was obvious to me that she had had a few too many. I found a seat at the bar and sat down.

The bartender came over and asked, "What would you like?" I smiled and ordered a light beer on tap. As he brought the glass over to me, he extended his hand and said, "I'm John, but you can call me Oates. That's what everybody calls me."

I shook his hand and said, "Hi! I'm Terry, glad to meet you Oats."

John asked, "Where you from?"

I answered, "I'm just cruising up and down the Mississippi, fishing and trying to stay out of trouble." He laughed and we talked for a few minutes, I learned that he and his younger sister owned the place.

John and I were swapping small talk when this beautiful young lady walked up to him behind the bar and said, "It's your turn." John turned around and introduced me to his little sister Cheryl. She shook my hand and I immediately felt my body start turning into putty as she took over as bartender. John excused himself and left. This young lady was more than beautiful; she was perfect in every way. She was maybe five foot two, had blonde hair with streaks of strawberry highlights, and she was perfectly proportioned, which the tight fitting tee shirt she was wearing proved very nicely. She had a smile that would light up the darkest room and my first thought was: Hit me, hurt me, use me, and make me write bad checks. As we talked I found out she used to be a cheerleader and gymnast in high school.

I was scheming and using my best lines on her when I heard the music start up again. I was just about to ask her if she was single when I heard Neal Diamond start singing "Red, red wine." I turned around and saw John on the stage with the mike in his hand. I couldn't believe it; he sounded more like Neal Diamond than Neal Diamond does. He was great! I was truly impressed. On any other night I could have listened to him sing all night long. But the song he chose started the memories of Catherine to start flooding back in again. I had already done this once today and even though I really didn't want to give up on my flirting with Cheryl, I didn't feel like doing it again. So I laid a ten-dollar bill on the bar, excused myself and headed back to the Pearl.

As I walked down the dock once more I thought to my self that I knew I never really stood a chance with John's little sister, but scheming on her was a lot of fun and she had seemed to enjoy the flirting as much as I did. It had also taken my mind off of other things. I smiled and lied to myself; "See, you still have what it takes, old man."

As I walked into the cabin and looked around at the small confined living room and kitchen that I called home, a feeling of true loneliness swept over me. The walls of the Pearl seemed to have closed in around me. I had been on my own and alone for many years now and I had become very comfortable with that. I needed no one close to me in order to confirm my self worth or make me feel happy. I had purposely steered away from relationships because they were just too much trouble. Always having to compromise my feelings to protect the other person's feelings. And when the relationship ended there was always the inevitable pain.

But all that was different now. With Catherine gone I didn't know how to be happy any more. I found myself searching for anything that would take my mind off of her. Nothing I was doing seemed to be enjoyable, not even the fishing. I longed just to see her face or hear her voice. Maybe it was because I had secluded myself for so many years, but tonight I was even questioning that precious self worth of mine. I had let her go without even the slightest resemblance of a fight. I had simply just walked away. Maybe it was the best thing I could have done for her, but it certainly wasn't the best for me. That was becoming too painfully clear tonight.

It was ten o'clock. I was wide-awake because of the nap I had taken earlier. I didn't want to drink any more. Even the taste of beer seemed to sour in my mouth. I had listened to all the music I could take for one day so I decided to watch TV for a while and hopefully find a good movie to take my mind off things again. As the television came on it was still on CNN. Anderson was just starting his broadcast and announced, "Now for the top story of the day. The Governor of Minnesota held a press conference this morning to share the news that his daughter, who had disappeared eighteen years ago, has been found alive."

The scene changed to a podium outside the capital building as Governor Redding stepped up to it and began to speak, "Ladies and gentleman, as a lot of you know, eighteen years ago our family lost one of our own. My daughter Catherine disappeared without a trace. We never did know what had happened to her, but last night she was returned to us alive and well. We now know what occurred on that terrible day. A man named Jean Paul Lafayette kidnapped Catherine. She was held against her will deep in the swamps of Louisiana. She would never have been heard from or seen again if it were not for a man that I personally owe my deepest gratitude. He not only found her, but he nursed her back to health, and helped her find her way back home. I can't say enough about this man. His caring and selflessness has made our family whole once more. He wouldn't accept any type of reward and doesn't wish to be pointed out for his acts, so I will not be providing any personal information about him. He knows who he is and all I can say is thank you. I will be working from home for the next week in order to spend time with my family and get to know my daughter again. I would appreciate it if the news media would respect our privacy and give us the time we need. My staff has all the details and will release them to you right after the press conference ends. In closing I would just like to apologize to all those good folks that took the time out of their busy schedules to come to the fund raiser last night. I'm sure they will forgive me for not being there and I'm sure they understand why. As it turned out, we all had a good evening. I got my daughter back and they got a good meal that didn't cost them a penny." Everyone there started laughing and cheering as the Governor left the podium. It was obvious that he was still running for President.

The scene changed back to Anderson as he continued his report. He said, "It seems there are two people that know the mystery man that the Governor was referring too."

The scene changed once more, this time to the marina. Tim and Troy were standing together very proudly talking to a reporter. The reporter asked, "Do you know who rescued and brought the Governors daughter back last night?"

Tim spoke up very quickly and said, "Oh yes, we know him very well. He's a very dear friend of ours."

Troy chimed in with, "And we know all about how he saved that lovely young girl from the clutches of that awful, awful man."

The reporter asked, "Can you give us his name?"

Tim and Troy looked at each other then back at the reporter as Tim answered, "Oh no, he's a very private individual and we simply cherish his friendship so we will be keeping that information to ourselves." Troy nodded in agreement. The two of them stood tall and smiled proudly into the camera.

I started laughing. I spoke out loud to the television as if Tim and Troy could hear me. Still chuckling I said, "You guys are all right. You rock." I flipped the channel over to a John Wayne movie and settled in for the night.

The next morning I was up and heading north even before the sun had come up. I spent the next four days exploring and fishing the lakes and rivers of Wisconsin and keeping to myself. I spent the nights anchored close to shores away from any marinas or populated areas. I wouldn't watch the news or listen to the radio in fear I might hear something that would get me thinking of Catherine again. That was a stupid plan. All I thought about was Catherine. But I did keep my cell phone close at all times. It was on that fourth morning that I realized that this was ridiculous. I was miserable and not even enjoying the fishing. I reeled in my line and walked into the cabin. I raised the anchors and started the engine. I needed to be around someone that cared for me and that I cared for. I decided to head back down to Newport, Mississippi, get in my Montero and go visit my son in Texas. I was sure a week or two with him was what I needed right now. I spun the wheel around and headed the Pearl south. I knew in my heart that I was doing the right thing. The Pearl could feel it too as she flew with the current back down the river.

It was amazing how fast the Pearl was traveling as she motored in unison with the current. We were making very good time even at half throttle. I put a Waylon Jennings CD on and sang with him about Texas as I smoked another cigarette and cruised down the river. My decision had me feeling much better now than I had in what seemed like a long time. I thought about calling my son to let him know I was coming, but then reconsidered and thought I would wait until I got closer to Newport I could be a little more accurate in telling him when I might be there. I figured that it took us ten days to get to St. Paul from Memphis against the current. Now that I would be traveling with the current it should only take about a week to get to Newport. I even entertained the idea of parking the Pearl at Stillwater and taking a bus to Texas. That would only take a day or so. I wouldn't have a car when I got there and would be dependant on my son to get around. I decided to stick with my first plan and go to Newport. The hours flew by and it was only about five as I neared Prescott again and would join up with the Mississippi. That's when my cell phone started ringing.

As I carefully took my cell phone out of my shirt pocket, I pressed the button and held it up to my ear. I meekly said, "Hello?"

A familiar voice answered, "Terry, this is Governor Redding, I'm not disturbing you am I?"

I quickly answered, "No sir, not at all. Is something wrong?" As I waited for a response I pulled the throttle all the way back, let the Pearl come to a stop and float down stream towards Prescott with the current.

The Governor answered, "No, nothing is wrong, everyone is fine. I called to see if you might be able to come back to St. Paul and see Catherine. She misses you a great deal and I feel it might help her if she could just spend some time with you again."

My heart started beating like a drum. I could hardly contain my emotions as I quickly told the Governor, "I can be back at the marina in about an hour and a half."

He said, "That would be great." He added, "I will have a car waiting for you at the docks."

As I hung up the phone I let out a loud Yahoo. I was coming to the Mississippi so I pushed the throttle forward all the way to full and turned the Pearl up towards the north. The Pearl hit the oncoming current with a vengeance and plowed ahead. She seemed to know how important this was and didn't seem to mind the extra stress I was putting on the engine.

The next hour and fifteen minutes seemed to crawl by. Every scenario I could imagine about what was going on ran through my head. I knew that there was a good chance of getting my heart broken again, but I didn't care. All that was important to me now was that I was going to see Catherine at least one more time. I felt like a schoolboy on a first date. My heart was racing and my knees even felt shaky as I headed the Pearl into the third street marina one more time.

The sun would be setting soon and I raced against time to get the Pearl tied down. As I finished securing her for the night I headed up the long wooden dock towards the shore. Tim and Troy came running out of the marina store and ran towards me screaming, "Terry you're back, you're back." As they reached me, they both turned around and each grabbed an arm and held onto me as the three of us hurried up towards the shoreline. As I reached the parking lot I could see Alex waiting for me next to a large black sedan. I excused myself to Tim and Troy and pulled my arms away and headed for the car.

As I got into the front seat next to him I asked, "Is Catherine all right?"

Alex just smiled, as we pulled away and simply stated, "She's fine." The ten-minute drive to the Governors mansion was made in complete silence. Alex didn't say a word; he just smiled as he drove.

When we finally reached the house, it seemed like it took forever for the security gates of the driveway to open. We parked just outside the garage. I unsnapped my seatbelt and quickly exited the car. I had to hold myself back from running as Alex and I walked towards the front door. As we finally reached the entrance, the maid was already holding the door open. As I entered the house Catherine was standing in the foyer waiting on me. She was the most beautiful creature I had ever seen. When she saw me she ran up and threw her arms around me pressing her lips to mine. I could have died a happy man just then. We embraced and kissed for what seemed a long time. The passion was overwhelming as I held her tightly in my arms once again.

When she finally did pull back she said, "I've missed you." The Governor and the First Lady walked up behind her. They were smiling and holding each other's hands. Still wrapped in my arms Catherine asked, "You once asked me to marry you. Do you still feel the same way?"

None of the scenarios that I had run through my mind as I had traveled up the river towards St. Paul had even come close to what was happening at this moment. It caught me by surprise. Without hesitation, and as I stared into those bright green eyes again, I answered, "There's nothing on earth that I want more."

Catherine pressed her lips against mine again, then pulling back she said, "Me either." I pulled her towards me and kissed her once more.

The Governor and First Lady stepped forward and pulled us apart. They were both laughing and the First Lady had tears running down her face as the Governor suggested we take this into the library. Catherine and I walked with them to the library holding on to one another very tightly. Alex followed as he always did. As we entered the room Alicia, Jesse and his wife were waiting. The Governor walked over to the bar and poured several glasses of cognac and then opened his humidor. As he passed out the drinks he handed Alex, Jesse and I a cigar. He raised his glass and said, "To Terry and Catherine, may they always be as happy as I am right now." As we all raised our glasses and answered the Governors toast, I knew he wasn't the happiest person in the room.

As we finished the toast, Catherine, still holding onto me tightly, looked at her father and said, "Daddy, you're the Governor, you have the power to marry us. Would you please do that for me right now?" I was surprised at Catherine's request, but I looked up at the Governor with complete support for her. The Governor stopped puffing on his cigar and looked at the First Lady. As they smiled at each other, he turned and looked back at us.

He said, "I've never been asked to perform a wedding before and to be honest with you, I have no idea how to do it. But if you will give me a few minutes to read up on it, I would be more than proud to marry the two of you." He added, "But if we do this, I think we should hold the ceremony on the boat." Catherine giggled and looked up at me with devious eyes, but I thought the Governor's idea was great. This whole thing had started on the Pearl and it was only fitting that our new life together should start there too.

As we all finished our drinks, the Governor closed the book he had gotten from his office and had been reading. He looked up at us all and said, "Ok, lets get this procession on its way." He started ushering everyone towards the garage. As we all piled into the long black limousine, everyone was laughing, and was in a very festive mood. All the guys were patting me on the back and all the women were kissing and hugging Catherine. Even Blackie seemed to be enjoying the moment. I could see that Alex, who was sitting in the front seat with the driver, even had a smile on his face. It became clear to me as we made the short trip to the marina, that Catherine and her family had been talking about and planning this together, long before I had arrived.

As we reached the marina and stepped from the limousine, I took Catherine's arm in mine and as I stared into her beautiful green eyes, started walking towards the Pearl. The Governor and the rest of the family started laughing. Finally the Governor yelled, "No Terry, this way." And they all headed down to another dock. I was confused but Catherine pulled at my arm, smiling, and we followed them. As we walked down the long wooden dock, we came upon the most beautiful boat I had ever seen in my life. She was a two-story nautical masterpiece. She was twenty feet wide and at least a hundred feet long.

As Catherine and I stepped up onto the lower rear deck, the rest of the family was waiting. Suddenly Tim and Troy came bounding out of the massive sliding glass doors. Tim was carrying a tray full of glasses and Troy had a bucket of iced Champaign. Tim was yelling, "Surprise, surprise!" I looked around at the deck we were standing on. It was massive. It was twenty feet wide and at least that long. The deck itself was made of Teak finished to a very high gloss. There were padded lounge chairs with silk pillows that matched the table and chairs in the center. It had bamboo torches all around the brass railings, casting a very romantic light on the deck. There were live potted trees in all four corners. It was more than beautiful, it was breath taking. The Governor could see I was fascinated with the boat so he said, "Go ahead, and have a look around." I grabbed Catherine's arm and headed inside.

As we entered the living room, I was in shock. Not only was it very large but also looked better than the Governor's mansion. The carpet was a thick tan pile. The walls were a combination of oak paneling and printed velour. There was an entertainment center to die for, with a sixty-inch flat screen TV. The chandelier looked like crystal glass. The couches and other furniture matched the design of the lounge chairs on the deck. As we continued, we walked through a formal dinning room with a full wet bar into a full size kitchen. The cabinets were all oak and the counter tops were marble. There was an oversized refrigerator freezer and a large stove with a microwave oven in the hood vent. As we continued down the hallway, there were three full size staterooms, each with their own full size bathrooms. Catherine was still giggling as we walked up the stairs to the second floor.

There was a large circular wheelhouse with a spectacular one hundred and eighty degree view. The helm was loaded with all the technology you could ask for. Radar, sonar, if you could name it, the instrument panel had it. Behind the wheelhouse was the most luxurious master bedroom I have ever seen. It was the full twenty feet wide by at least thirty feet long. There was a king size bed in the center of the room with solid oak night stands that matched the mirrored dresser and mans wardrobe cabinet. There were two large walk-in closets and a beautiful full size bathroom with a separate shower and a large Jacuzzi style bathtub. We continued out the back sliding glass doors to a smaller, but beautiful, open-air rear deck. The deck was the same Teak as down stairs and the furniture matched that of the master bedroom design. There was a large lighted Jacuzzi in the middle. We followed a stairway up to the top deck that covered the bedroom and wheelhouse below. There was patio furniture and a picnic table scattered around and up front was an open-air Fly bridge, so that the boat could be driven from up here. This was the most amazing floating mansion I had ever seen.

As Catherine and I walked back down stairs and joined the family on the rear lower deck, I said to the Governor, "This is quite a boat sir, have you had it long?"

The First Lady was holding on to the Governor's arm and they looked at each other and smiled. Then he turned his head back towards me and said, "Oh, this isn't my boat." Then he paused and still smiling, looked back at the First Lady. As I stood there with a dumb look on my face, Catherine was holding my arm, giggling and bouncing up and down as she look up at me smiling from ear to ear. The Governor slowly turned his head back towards me and extended his arm. He held out a set of keys and dropped them into my hand as he said, "It's not my boat it's yours." As I stood there in total shock with Catherine laughing and almost pulling my arm off, he continued, "You deserve it." The rest of the family including Tim and Troy started yelling and clapping. Troy popped the cork on the Champaign bottle and started pouring drinks for everyone. I didn't know what to do or say, I just stood there looking like an idiot.

The Champaign was flowing and the party had started in earnest. The Governor let go of the First Lady's arm and raised his hands high into the air with his palms flat, waving them up and down. He yelled, "Ok, lets quiet it down a little, we still have some serious matters to take care of before we all get too carried away." At that prompt, the First Lady slid over next to Catherine. Jesse walked over and stood next to me. The Governor cleared his throat, and then asked, "Do we have the ring?" Jesse reached into his pocket, pulled out a velvet-covered box, and opened it. Inside was a beautiful diamond wedding ring. I laughed out loud and thought to myself, *how much do you want to bet that it's an exact fit for Catherine's finger.* The Governor took out his book and started the ceremony. Troy, as he held on to Tim's arm, started to cry and Tim started sniffling. The Governor read what love was really all about, but I didn't hear a word. All I could do was look into those bright green eyes and smile.

When he reached the part about do you Terry, I waited for him to finish then said, "I do."

He turned to Catherine and asked her if she… and before he could finish Catherine said, "I do."

The Governor, feeling Catherine's excitement, sped up his reading and had me put the ring on her finger. I was right. It was a perfect fit. Then he quickly added, "With the powers vested in me as Governor of the State of Minnesota, I now pronounce you man and wife. You may kiss the bride." I did.

Everyone started clapping and yelling. The First Lady with tears in her eyes, held Catherine tightly and kissed her cheek. Jesse shook my hand then the Governor slapped me on the shoulder and said, "Welcome to the family son." Tim had tears in his eyes and was trying to console Troy whose head was now on Tim's shoulder as he balled like a baby. Blackie started howling and Alex stood at the sliding glass doors in his normal stance, smiling.

The Governor raised his hands once more and quieted everyone down again. He pulled an envelope from underneath his jacket and handed it to Catherine and me. As I opened it he said, "Just a little something from your mother and me." This was obviously something Catherine had no idea about because her mouth dropped as low as mine did when we saw the check for one million dollars. The party went into high gear after that and lasted until well after one in the morning. When it did finally come to an end and the last person to leave stepped onto the dock, Catherine and I smiled at each other and headed up stairs to our new bedroom.

The next morning I awoke to the sound of seagulls screeching above the river. The sun was just starting to peek through the curtains. Catherine and I were still wrapped in each other's arms, lying in the middle of that enormous bed. As I lay there watching her sleep, I couldn't believe how lucky I was. When her eyes finally started to open, she smiled at me with a loving look that melted my very soul. I smiled and said, "Good morning, Mrs. Stevens. How would you like to spend your honeymoon in Key West?" She smiled and gently pulled my head down to hers. The kiss was long and passionate. We didn't crawl out of bed for another hour. As we got up to take our showers, we held each other close and walked into the bathroom to begin the day together.

Catherine and I spent the day getting ready to head out for Key West the next morning. I called a painting crew in and, in gold leaf lettering, had the name CATHERINE painted on the back of the new boat. We spent the rest of the day getting things out of the Pearl, putting them away on the Catherine, and stocking it with supplies. We had a carpenter install doggie doors and had the nursery lay blue grass sod on the small front deck for Blackie. I sold the Pearl to Tim and Troy knowing they would take very good care of her. The First Lady kept Alicia out of school and the two of them helped us get every thing ready to go.

As the next morning arrived, the entire family was there to see us off. The paparazzi had filled the parking lot snapping pictures with their very long lenses. The Governor gave me a humidor full of Cohiba cigars. He made Catherine promise to call him every day. The First Lady was crying and hugging Catherine every chance she got. Alicia and Jesse both hugged and wished us the best honeymoon ever. Catherine and I said our goodbyes and headed up to the top deck Fly bridge and fired up the engines. As we pulled out on to the river everyone on shore was waving and Catherine was crying and waving back. As we made our turn south, we saw Tim and Troy sipping strawberry daiquiris on the back yard of the Pearl. It was Tuesday and everyone knew that they always had daiquiris on Tuesdays. They were just getting an early start. They raised their glasses high as we passed and I blew the horn twice to signal goodbye. Catherine came up and took my arm. I smiled as I looked at her and said, "You know, with all that has happened in the last few months, we should write a book about it." We stared at each other smiling for a moment and then we laughed, shook our heads, and at the same time said, "No, who would believe us." As we sailed down the river towards the Gulf of Mexico, Alex stood guard in his usual fashion on the rear lower deck watching out over CATHERINE.

The beginning.

Printed in the United States
202755BV00002B/1-51/P